"Sorry. You're not my type." Maggie dismissed him.

"Funny, from the way you were looking at me a couple of minutes ago, I thought I was exactly your type," Jake said.

"Well, you were wrong!" Maggie fumed as she stepped back swiftly and came up against a post. "What I want is a husband, not a hot-blooded lover."

"Why not? I might not be in the market for a wife, but I sure enjoy a toss in the hay every now and then." He quickly hauled her into his arms.

Maggie didn't know how it happened. As his hot, clever lips wrenched an unwilling response from her, she began to feel as if there was only this moment, this man....

Dear Reader,

Picture this: You're thirty, single and on a husband hunt! You've done your research, highlighted the eligible bachelors, made lists and spreadsheets, bar graphs and flow charts...and you've narrowed your choices down to a millionaire, a cowboy and the boy next door.

That's exactly what three American Romance heroines have done—and we're about to pick up their stories in the hilarious HOW TO MARRY... trilogy. Here, Cathy Gillen Thacker introduces you to the second bride-in-waiting, who has her eye on *One Hot Cowboy*. Don't miss *The Bad Boy Next Door* next month, from Mindy Neff.

Find out if these three men can show these three women a thing or two about passion—the most important part of a marriage!

Happy reading!

Debra Matteucci
Senior Editor & Editorial Coordinator
Harlequin Books
300 East 42nd Street
New York, NY 10017

# HOW TO MARRY...

# ONE HOT COWBOY

*Cathy Gillen Thacker*

# Harlequin Books

TORONTO • NEW YORK • LONDON
AMSTERDAM • PARIS • SYDNEY • HAMBURG
STOCKHOLM • ATHENS • TOKYO • MILAN
MADRID • WARSAW • BUDAPEST • AUCKLAND

ISBN 0-373-16673-7

ONE HOT COWBOY

Copyright © 1997 by Cathy Gillen Thacker.

**Printed in U.S.A.**

# *Prologue*

"There's no way I can change your mind?" Peter Lassiter asked unhappily as Maggie Porter watched the movers carry the last of her boxes to the truck parked on the Manhattan street below.

Maggie smiled at the debonair owner of the Lassiter Modeling Agency. "None," she said cheerfully. Peter had given her her start as a supermodel. Fit and trim, and elegantly attired in a suit and tie, the preppy sandy-haired agent was one of the funniest and savviest men Maggie had ever met. And the most fickle. With an unerring eye for physical beauty, he fell passionately in and out of love at least three times a year, and was chased fervently by aspiring models on a daily basis.

"You're sure?"

Maggie gave him a patient look as she moved her airline ticket, suitcase, album of precious photos and handbag out of harm's way. "I wouldn't have arranged to put my belongings in storage and sold my apartment if I wasn't," she told him seriously. As of today, September 1, she was free of all contractual obligations.

"I still think you're making a mistake," Peter confided in a husky whisper. "So you're thirty, so what. Ten years ago you might have been over-the-hill in this business, but now America is aging and so are the cover models. No one graces a magazine cover better than you do, Maggie. With the way you've taken care of yourself, you still have at least two or three stupendously successful years left." Peter paused, allowing time for his words to sink in. "You could make several million more dollars in that time. From there, go on to be a celebrity spokesperson or entertainment and fashion reporter. There's no reason for you to leave the industry altogether."

Maggie was well aware of the path other supermodels had taken; it wasn't for her. It was time for her to be more than a pretty face or a spectacular body. Past time, really. She held up a well-manicured hand. "I have enough money, Peter, more than enough to last me a lifetime. What I need now is a life."

"You have one here," Peter persisted.

Maggie shook her head as the movers returned and then departed with her sofa, two chairs and an end table. She wasn't talking about filling up every spare minute of the day with well-paying bookings, arduous workouts and endless rounds of parties; she was talking about feeling content at the end of the day, about feeling loved, needed, wanted, about having a family of her own.

"I know I have a life here. And on the surface anyway, it's been a good one, Peter. It's just not the kind I want." Not anymore.

"SO THE DEED is done?" Maggie's cousin Hallie Fortune asked long-distance, after Peter had finally given up and left. Hallie and Maggie had been close since childhood, when Maggie's family had spent several weeks every summer in Chicago with Hallie's family, and Hallie's family had visited with Maggie's family in Texas, every winter.

Maggie sat cross-legged on the bare wood floor, her back against the sun-warmed windowsill. "They've moved me out lock, stock and barrel. I've arranged for my phone and utilities to be turned off tomorrow. So all I have left to do is hand over my keys to the new owners and take one last look around the old neighborhood before heading to my brother's place in Texas. He's putting me up until I decide where and with whom I want to settle down."

"You speak as if you expect that to happen fairly soon," Hallie noted, with the insight of a trusted confidante.

Cradling the phone between her shoulder and ear, Maggie tugged on her buff-colored western boots. "That's because I do."

"I wish I had your faith in fairy-tale endings," Hallie, an only child who'd had a tumultuous childhood, said wistfully.

"Who said anything about fairy-tale endings?" Maggie retorted, knowing she and her younger brothers had had to fight tooth and nail for everything they'd managed to achieve since their parents had died when she was nineteen. "I have given up on waiting for Mr. Right to just happen to stumble into my path. These days, I'm taking destiny into my own hands, and—to borrow a phrase from my football coach brother—running with it."

"Now that sounds ominous," Hallie said, a hint of humor creeping into her low melodious voice, before she demanded protectively, "What exactly are you planning to do?"

"Change my life." That said, Maggie tugged the brim of her Yankee baseball cap lower over her brow, then put on a pair of round wire-rimmed sunglasses. "I'm going back to Texas to find myself a husband and have that family I've always wanted."

"And to aid you, I imagine you've still got your famous wish list that you hold all potential suitors up against?" Hallie said with a chuckle.

Maggie flushed slightly but took no offense. "You bet I do!" she replied enthusiastically, as she stood and smoothed the soft fabric of her washed-out bolero jacket over her white T-shirt and faded jeans.

Mentally consulting her famous wish list, she began to pace. "I want someone smart and funny and willing and wise. He's got to be handy around the house, and want to be a good father. He needs to be tall, 'cause I like tall men. Built. Rugged, in that kind of capable outdoorsy way. Dark-haired."

"I suppose you've even figured out your potential husband's eye color," Hallie teased.

Maggie sighed wistfully as she touched a hand to the bouncy ponytail escaping through the clasp of her cap. With a sigh, she admitted dreamily, "Blue, if I get my preference, but I could live with green or brown or even gray, so long as he has that kind of determined hell-bent-for-leather look about him, whenever he sets out to accomplish something, big or small, and that includes winning my heart."

"You're going to make him work for your hand in marriage, I suppose?" Hallie prodded.

"But of course." Maggie laughed, anticipating the thrill of a courtship that would lead to the romance that would last her whole life. She picked up her photo album and thumbed through the pages, until she came to the photo of Hallie, Clarissa and herself standing in front of a fortune-teller's tent at the SummerFest when they were all twelve. Maggie grinned, seeing the green lizard in her hands that she'd won at the shooting booth. What a tomboy she'd been then, and still was, at heart! "Of course, my Mr. Right has also got to know how to sit a horse, and toss a ball around, and snow ski, and swim, and maybe do a little ropin' and ridin', too," Maggie continued firmly, "'cause I intend to follow in my brother Deke's footsteps and raise my kids on a ranch."

"A cowboy, hmm?" Hallie prodded.

"A Texas cowboy," Maggie specified with pride as she mentioned her home state with undisguised yearning, "and yes, that would be best, since Texas is where I intend to settle, now that I am getting out of the modeling business, once and for all." She couldn't wait to be back in the wide open spaces, beneath the bright blue sky.

Intrigued, Hallie sighed. "You know how you're going to go about this, I suppose?" she queried dryly.

"Of course." Maggie smiled and held the receiver a little closer to her ear. "You know I never embark on anything without a plan!"

Silence fell between the two cousins.

"You going to tell me what you have up your

sleeve or make me pry it out of you?'' Hallie drawled
finally.

''You'll poke fun at me,'' Maggie predicted.

''Probably,'' Hallie countered, amiably enough.
''I'd still like to know.''

Just then a taxi horn blared and a string of profan-
ities that would cause a longshoreman to blush followed on the Manhattan street below. Maggie couldn't
wait to put the nonstop noise and pollution of the city
behind her and head back to the peaceful beauty of
Texas ranch land, and the sure, sweet simplicity of
family life. ''The way I see it, the whole problem with
romance is the randomness of it all. I mean, my work
has taken me all over the world. I've met and dated
all sorts of extremely eligible men, and I still haven't
found my Mr. Right,'' Maggie said sadly.

For a while, two years previously, she'd thought she
had. But to her dismay, that romance had turned out
to be as false and superficial as the life she'd been
living. And when it had ended she'd felt more disillusioned and alone than ever. So much so, in fact, that
she had known that her life, and the way she was
going about things, had to change.

''So…?'' Hallie prodded.

''So after careful thought and consideration, it oc-
curred to me that relying on something as flimsy and
*un*reliable as mere fate to put me in the right place at
the right time with the right man is not working out.
I have to start doing what the magnificent Sabrina advised when we were kids, and make my own destiny.''
Maggie paused. ''Not that Sabrina knew everything,''
she amended hastily.

"Because if she had," Hallie agreed, "we'd probably all be married by now."

"Right. Me to a cowboy, Clarissa to a millionaire and you to your next-door neighbor, Cody Brock."

Hallie groaned with heartfelt chagrin. "Don't remind me of that prediction. I'm still trying to live it down."

Maggie smiled, then unable to resist, asked, "Is he still a hellion, by the way?"

Another silence. "As far as I know." Hallie sighed, with what sounded like genuine lament. "To tell you the truth, I can't imagine him ever changing."

"I know that feeling," Maggie agreed. The New York modeling world—where the emphasis was on how you looked not who you were—was not about to change, either. And that was why she had to get out. Go back to her roots. To a life with more meaning, more joy. To a life with love that was deep and real and would last a lifetime.

"Besides," Maggie continued, getting back to the immediate subject. "I don't believe anyone can predict the future, which is another reason why I'm taking fate into my own hands," she said with Texas-style determination. "I'm going to find myself the cowboy of my dreams, throw a rope around him and reel him in." And she'd do it all before he ever knew what hit him.

Hallie laughed softly. "Clarissa and I always did admire your gumption, Maggie."

"Speaking of Clarissa, have you heard from her lately?" For years the three of them had been as close as sisters. As teens, they'd hung out together and attended the Chicago SummerFest every year, when Maggie visited from Texas.

"No," Hallie said, sounding troubled. "You?"

"Not for several months." Maggie paused. "She hasn't been returning my calls or answering my letters." Though she had never liked or trusted Clarissa McShaunessy's husband, Clarissa's seven-year-old son Tommy was an angel; she missed hearing about him on a regular basis.

"Mine, either. I recommended her for a teaching job at the Latin School in Chicago, but I haven't heard from her since then."

Maggie continued to pace back and forth, worried. "You don't think something is wrong, do you?"

"Surely she would've called us—" Hallie said, then stopped.

"Unless she was embarrassed." Maggie sighed "You know how she hates for people to feel sorry for her." Clarissa McShaunessy had been passed around from one uncaring relative to another, after being orphaned at a young age. Proud and sensitive, she'd been forced to live through one indignity after another. Though beautiful, she had no choice but to wear outdated, ill-fitting hand-me-downs the other children had ridiculed. She'd never gone to school with enough lunch money. Never had anything to call her own. Yet she had worked like crazy to earn her keep with whatever indifferent relative she had lived.

"Last I heard she was in Philadelphia," Hallie said. "But you know how frequently she and her husband move."

"Whenever he gets a new job." Or loses one, Maggie thought. "Well, maybe she'll call or write us. In the meantime, we'll keep trying to reach her."

"Agreed," Hallie said. "Now, back to your situation."

"I was hoping you'd forgotten." No one grilled her like the ever-practical, ever-efficient Hallie.

"Not a chance," Hallie said firmly. "Let's hear your plans for hunting your Mr. Downright-Perfect!"

Maggie drew an enervating breath and told all. "I've decided to research men the way I once researched colleges and modeling agencies, and find a list of men who not only possess all the qualities on my wish list, but are also every bit as successful as I am in my own right, and then go after them one by one, until the chemistry is right and everything clicks and I finally find my dream man."

In fact, her plan was so simple, she didn't know why she hadn't thought of it earlier. A businesslike approach to problems always brought about a quick solution; she knew that from experience.

Hallie was plainly skeptical—maybe because she was a nurse—and whether by profession or nature, was much more intuitively connected to people's needs. "You really think this is going to work?" Hallie asked incredulously.

Maggie smiled. "It's so logical, it has to work." she retorted confidently. "I mean, somewhere out there, there has to be a man my age who's not just meant for me, in that once-in-a-lifetime way, but who is every bit as ready to fall in love with me as I am with him. All I have to do is find him, Hallie. And then put myself in the right place at the right time, and meet him, and voilà, the true love we feel for each other will take it from there.''

AFTER SHE HUNG UP the phone, and with a good hour and a half before she had to turn over the key to her apartment to the new owners, Maggie decided to take one last look around the neighborhood. She stepped out onto the crowded Village street she had called home for the last ten years. A holiday weekend, the normally busy area was eerily quiet, almost unnaturally so, Maggie thought. The sun was making its way toward the horizon as a breeze floated across the tree-lined street. The evening air was balmy and just cool enough to hint at the autumn to come. Maggie passed an art gallery, and a produce store—both of which were closed—and headed toward the deli on the corner.

It was 7:00 p.m., and she was famished. Halfway down the block, she paused as she noticed a newly painted sign hanging from the lamppost above the storefront. Fortunes Told By Sabrina, it said.

Maggie stopped dead in her tracks. Funny, how she and Hallie had just spoken about the gypsy. But this Sabrina couldn't be the same Sabrina she had seen at the Chicago fair some eighteen years ago, could it? Then again, how many fortune-tellers were there named Sabrina?

Deciding to take a trip down memory lane, Maggie opened the door to the once empty building and stepped inside. The shades were drawn and the beguiling scent of incense filled the shop. A dark-eyed woman smiled at Maggie warmly and clasped her gnarled hands. "Come in, Maggie darling, come in."

Maggie blinked. The clothes weren't the same. But the heavy jewelry, the kind, kohl-rimmed eyes and hauntingly omniscient smile were the same. "Sabrina?" Maggie gasped as a wealth of memories assaulted her. Merciful heavens, it was her!

The fortune-teller nodded as she swept forward. "I see you remember me."

As Sabrina led her toward a cloth-draped table, with a huge crystal ball in the center of it, Maggie let out the breath she had been holding. "You read my palm and told my fortune. And told me we all make our own destiny in this life."

"That's right." Sabrina smiled gently as she ushered Maggie into a chair. "There have been many changes in your life since then, haven't there?"

Maggie sat down before she fell down. "That's putting it mildly."

"But still no man in your life." Sabrina shook her head.

Maggie leveled a curious look at the fortune-teller. What timing, to have Sabrina come back into her life now, Maggie thought. "You said I'd marry a cowboy."

"And you shall." Sabrina studied her. "You are skeptical?"

Maggie shrugged her shoulders. "I admit it all seemed magical when I was a kid," she allowed. "It still does. But as for anyone having the power to see into the future..." Maggie's voice trailed off. "I'm sorry, Sabrina, I don't mean to offend you, but I just don't believe in palm reading."

Sabrina smiled. "That is all right, Maggie. But indulge me as I gaze into my crystal ball," she said as she waved her hands over the top and sides of the sphere. As they peered down into it, Sabrina spoke of a startlingly beautiful vista. Maggie knew at once, by the description of the stark flat landscape, the acres of dark brown fence and Brahma cattle, that it was Texas. Though she only saw the warped reflection of the paisley tablecloth through the orb.

"In the distance, I see an outcropping of trees." Then Sabrina became serious, frighteningly so. "Beneath it, a wreath of well-tended flowers surrounding a fenced-in area with two graves." A chill went down Maggie's spine. Was this her resting place she was seeing? Was Sabrina predicting her death?

"Your fate is already decided," Sabrina told Maggie. "I see him. A tall, broad-shouldered man in a Stetson, lingering outside the white picket fence that surrounds the graves...now he is gone...another image is appearing...it is becoming clearer...yes, yes, now I see you, Maggie."

Thoroughly caught up, Maggie leaned this way and that. But try as she might, she could not see what Sabrina was describing. "And now you and this cowboy, together."

Maggie accepted that the whole hocus-pocus atmosphere was just a bit of gimmickry, drawn from Maggie's long-ago professed desire to marry a cowboy, and her recent, very public proclamations that she was retiring from modeling and returning to her native Texas.

Sabrina gazed raptly into the crystal ball. "I have much work to do," she murmured softly. "Not just for you, Maggie, but for Hallie and Clarissa, too—wait." Sabrina waved her hands over the murky surface of the crystal ball. "Another image is appearing," she murmured urgently.

The practical side of Maggie knew this was all nonsense; nevertheless, she was on the edge of her seat, trying to see what Sabrina was seeing, if for no other reason than to satisfy her own considerable curiosity. "Is it Texas again?" Maggie persisted, for it was clear from the utterly mesmerized look on Sabrina's face that Sabrina was seeing something.

Sabrina nodded. "You will marry a man and have many children with him...half a dozen, in fact. Some with light hair, some with dark...." Sabrina paused, frowning.

"But there's a catch, right?" Maggie said, aware she was as captivated by all this as she was mistrusting.

Sabrina nodded, affirming this to be true. Her voice dropped a mesmerizing notch.

"First, you must mend his broken heart."

# Chapter One

He caught sight of her on the video surveillance monitor mounted on the dash of his pickup truck, slipping through a little-known side gate and onto the Rollicking M Ranch as though she not only owned the place, but knew it well.

She was wearing a flat-brimmed straw hat to ward off the September sunshine, dark denim figure-hugging jeans, a white cotton blouse with a narrow band collar, and a vest in the same caramel hues as her knee-high western boots.

A smile of anticipation curving her full lips, she guided her horse through the golden Texas meadow with the easy grace of an expert rider. She was, he thought in bemusement, completely unaware she had tripped the silent alarm and her image had been picked up and transmitted via state-of-the-art color monitors to several locations on the ranch.

Beside him, the shortwave radio crackled before Harry Wholesome's deep voice boomed, "We've got company."

"I know," he grumbled back, wishing for the millionth time that great wealth **did** not attract such lunatics—even the stunningly beautiful ones. "I see her." *I may wish I didn't, but I see her.*

He studied the woman's model-perfect features and pale golden hair. Damn, she was a looker. Tall. Slender. With gently curving breasts, a trim waist, and long sexy legs. Clearly, she was the most beautiful—and widely photographed—intruder they'd had yet. What she didn't know was that he and Harry and the rest of the ranch hands had been tipped off by a photographer at the Houston newspaper, and had been expecting her to show up.

Unfortunately, he was not in the mood for this. He'd spent the morning halterbreaking a colt no one else was having any luck with, including him as it turned out, then fine-tuning the funny little rattle out of the engine on Harry's pickup. Which was what he got for being a jack-of-all-trades, he supposed wearily—all the jobs on the ranch no one else wanted. Though they'd be standing in line for this one, he thought with a shimmer of heartfelt anticipation, still watching the woman pick her way through the field of rippling yellow grass.

Especially since, two years after her much-publicized engagement to a New York City real estate developer had ended with a whimper instead of a wedding ceremony, she was very much on the lookout for a new man. Reportedly a wealthy native Texan this time, like herself.

Course, he could—on some level—understand that, too. The trespassing supermodel knew her looks would not be bringing in the big bucks forever. At age thirty, she had a couple good years left, and then she'd be on the downside of the money curve. Which was also no doubt why she'd made such a big splash announcing her "retirement" in the press. She probably wanted to be lured back temporarily by the best money she'd earn yet. Though the grandstanding ploy might work, it was all pretty shallow, in his opinion. As no doubt, was she.

On the other end of the shortwave, Harry sighed impatiently. "Want me to cut this little episode short and call the sheriff?" he barked, ready to take action, as soon as he got the okay.

His gut tightened as he continued to watch her. He didn't know what it was about her—but he understood why she was so successful. He couldn't take his eyes off her. He doubted any other man could either.

"No. I'll take care of it," he volunteered reluctantly, tossing down his work gloves and watching as the intruder guided her mount swiftly up over the rise and headed for the sprawling hacienda-style ranch house, with its white stucco walls and red tile roof.

Women had been breaching the MacIntyre domain for years, but never, he thought, as the beautiful woman dismounted, pulled something from the top of her boot, and covertly reached for her mare's right foreleg, as brazenly as this!

Continuing to watch her fiddle knowingly with her horse's shoe, he shook his head and grinned. Considering the caculatedness of her actions, perhaps it was time he traded this pickup for a horse and taught her a lesson of which Old Man MacIntyre was sure to approve.

ALTHOUGH SHE WAS pretending mightily to be a perplexed damsel in distress as she knelt next to her borrowed palomino, crooning softly and petting Buttercup all the while, Maggie spotted the down-and-out ranch hand on the spotted Appaloosa the moment he topped the rise.

In a sweat-stained denim shirt and jeans, disreputable-looking boots and hat, he sat his horse in a lazy, all-male way that made her throat go dry. As he closed in on her, she could see he was covered from head to toe with a fine film of ranch dust and a few splatters of black grease.

He was handsome, his deeply suntanned face sexy, his square even features slightly angular. But the dark stubble clinging to his jaw, coupled with his thick brown mustache and the calmly assessing glint in his deep chocolate brown eyes, only added to his dangerous appearance.

"Just as I thought," the sexy cowboy drawled, swinging lithely off of the saddle. Letting go the reins, he shook his head at Maggie in a way that immediately gave her second thoughts about her plan. Still looking her up and down, his gaze covering every inch of her, he swept off his dusty Stetson and slapped it against one thigh. "The boss is not going to like this."

She had no choice but to brazen it out, even as she took in his rumpled sable brown hair and a face that had not seen a razor for several days. She gave him the smile that had graced many a magazine cover over the years. "The fact my horse lost a shoe?" she asked.

The cowboy set his hat on his head and tugged it low on his brow. He smoothed the ends of his thick mustache and gave her a warning look that was very much at odds with the heat in his eyes. "The fact you're trespassing," he replied.

Something about the way the disreputable cowboy was looking at her—as if she were a dessert he was dying to taste—caused her pulse to quicken. "Jake MacIntyre is that mean?" Maggie asked.

"And then some, I'd say," the sexy cowboy intoned, moving closer yet.

Maggie looked past him, at the sprawling hacienda-style ranch house. A place this big was bound to have multiple employees. Surely, someone else would come along soon. Maybe even Jake MacIntyre! The reclusive rancher she'd heard about. All she had to do was stall. "You work this ranch?" she asked, as they continued to square off.

The cowboy knelt next to Buttercup and examined her newly unshod foot. "Certainly looks that way, don't it," he murmured, next examining the smooth, relatively unscathed horsehoe on the ground. He frowned. "If I didn't know better, I'd think this shoe was pulled off!"

Damn, but this cowboy was trouble with a capital *T*. Never one to throw in the towel, especially on a battle she could win, Maggie decided to give back as good as she was getting. "Of course it was pulled off," she admitted brazenly, her cheeks pinkening slightly even as she held the cowboy's steady, probing gaze. "I pulled it off after it became loose and nearly fell off. I didn't want poor Buttercup tripping and stumbling over a loose shoe. She might've pulled a tendon."

"Well, now, that was mighty considerate of you," he drawled, the devil in his eyes. His eyes still locked with hers, he stood again and towered over her. Which wasn't easy, Maggie thought. Considering that the heels of their boots were each about two inches thick, he had a good six inches on her, which made him at least six feet six inches. A very handsome and imposing six feet six inches.

"Thank you," Maggie murmured, turning her eyes from him.

"Oh, you're welcome."

Desperate to move his attention away from her horse, Maggie turned the conversation back to him. "You look like you've had a hard day, too. Your clothes, and all," she added hastily, as her glance moved over his solidly muscled chest.

The Rollicking M cowboy lifted a brow. He rolled his weight from his heels to his toes, until he was leaning over her, emanating warmth. "That's what happens when you put in an *honest* day's work," he told her significantly.

Maggie caught the hint of derision in his tone, even as she breathed in the salty tang of his sweat, mingling with the lingering scent of soap and cologne, from a shower she guessed he had taken just hours ago.

She wondered why he hadn't bothered to shave, too, even as she propped her hands on her hips and squared off with him. "You probably think I don't know anything about that," she accused.

He shrugged and regarded her facetiously from beneath the shadowy brim of his hat. He gave her a taunting half smile. "Not up to me to say, lady, one way or 'nother."

"Well, I do know," Maggie continued, offended. She would not have people say she'd had an easy time of it. Modeling was hard, often grueling, work. She had earned every penny she had made and then some.

"I have supported myself for years! I put myself and my brothers through college, too."

He looked her up and down, taking his time about it, before returning his insultingly frank gaze to her face. Locking eyes with her, he grinned what by now had become a most infuriating smirk.

"I'll have to take your word on that, now, won't I?" he drawled.

Maggie blew out an exasperated breath. "You surely will."

Apparently able to tell he had insulted her, the cowboy slapped a hand dramatically across his chest. "Don't get me wrong. I think, from what I've seen of it, and I've seen a lot here on the Rollicking M, that fortune hunting is damn hard work. In fact, it's a lot sweatier and dirtier than anything I've done today," he continued.

Maggie swore inwardly and damned him for catching on to her plan so quickly, even though it was none of his business. "What gives you the idea I'm fortune hunting?" Maggie demanded coolly, knowing full well, even if this cowboy didn't, that she was looking for love, not money. And she wouldn't even be doing *that* if it had come her way naturally, as she had long and often wished.

"Oh, it's easy enough to figure out, when you show up here like this, dressed to kill."

Maggie swept a hand down the simple but very attractive Western attire she'd spent hours selecting this morning. "This?" She shrugged off his backhanded compliment with the same unchecked audacity with which it had been given. "This is nothing." *You ought to see me in Armani or Donna Karan.*

His sable brown eyes darkened unhappily. An Arctic chill wafted between them. Maggie decided they had traded barbs long enough. "Is there a blacksmith on the ranch who can reshoe my horse?"

Looking equally ready to escape from her, the cowboy scowled at her, then at Buttercup. "The Rollicking M does not employ its own blacksmith—"

"A phone then."

His powerful shoulders strained against the damp denim fabric of his shirt. "We got one you could use in the stables."

*Perfect*, Maggie thought.

Reading her mind, he continued lazily, "which, by the way, are located well away from the main house."

*Not so perfect.* Realizing what he was hinting at, Maggie decided to tackle the subject of her trustworthiness head-on. Tilting her chin at him, she asked, "What's the problem, cowboy? Think I'll steal your boss's china?"

The sexy cowboy shook his head and taunted her with an insolent grin. "Not very damn likely, with Harry Wholesome around."

Maggie focused for a moment on the thin but sensual curve of his lips before returning to his dark-lashed brown eyes. It was a shame his eyes weren't blue, and that he had a mustache; otherwise he was about perfect, as far as the physical requirements of her wish list went anyway. The personality section was another matter. On that, he needed a major overhaul.

"Who's Harry?"

"The majordomo of the Rollicking M Ranch."

Maggie blinked and, aware her heart was racing

again, stepped back a pace. "Jake MacIntyre has a male housekeeper?"

He gave her a cynical look. "Surprised?"

"Maybe. A little."

"Why?"

"I don't know." Maggie shrugged. "I just figured, a single guy, he'd have a woman working for him."

"Well, you figured wrong. He doesn't want women underfoot, particularly young single ones."

Maggie hadn't climbed to the top of the New York modeling trade without knowing how to take advantage of an opportunity. "Perhaps I should apologize to him in person then," she suggested breezily.

"What for?"

"What else?" Maggie spread her hands wide. "Intruding on his privacy."

"Two wrongs don't make a right."

"Now see here, Mr.—"

"You can call me J.D., if you want."

"It's not wrong to apologize," Maggie continued with an indignant sniff.

"Trust me," he said with a smug, knowing look. "In this case, considering how and why you happen to be here like this, it would be." He hunkered down beside Buttercup and examining both her unshod foot and hoof and then the thrown horseshoe, shook his head. "I just don't get it," he murmured.

"Don't get what?" Maggie asked uncomfortably, wondering just how much this J.D. guessed or knew about her plan.

He shook his head again. "Usually when a horse throws a shoe, it's because it is a little worn down, or maybe damaged in some way. This one looks fine, except for being off. Plus," J.D. moved around and checked all Buttercup's shoes in turn in excrutiating detail while Maggie restlessly shifted her weight from foot to foot, "the others are all on tight as a drum." He shoved back his hat with the tip of his finger. Chocolate brown eyes dancing, he peered down at her. "How do you reckon this shoe might've gotten loosened to the point where you had to take it off for the horse's safety, Miss—?"

"Porter. Maggie Porter. And I'm certain I couldn't tell you," Maggie said stiffly, furious he kept returning to this anomaly when she was damn sure he knew that she would rather he not dwell on it.

"Hmm. Well, I suppose I'll have to think about that. Nothing like a mystery just waiting to be solved. Meantime, I suppose we better head on back to the barn, if we're going to get this fixed. Course, you can't ride your horse, with her missing shoe," J.D. remarked. "We'll have to lead her."

"Fine," Maggie said impatiently. "It's not far anyway."

She watched him take the reins of her horse, then gaped as he swung himself up in the saddle of his Appaloosa. She had expected him to walk along beside her and the horses, not ride while she walked.

J.D. leaned across his saddle and put a hand down to her. "C'mon," he said, tucking the thrown shoe into his saddlebag, and motioning her up onto his horse with a nod of his head. "Let's go."

Maggie blinked in surprise. "You want me to ride your horse, too?"

"Would appear so, wouldn't it?" he drawled, rolling his eyes.

Maggie bit her lip. She couldn't imagine being that close to him. Plus, doing so might mean inadvertently transferring some of the dust and grease on his clothes, to hers. "I don't know about this."

J.D. lifted his hat and resituated it squarely on his handsome head. "Lady, I ain't got all day," he warned, exasperated. "So either get yourself up here or eat my dust, if you get my point."

With the September sunshine beating down upon her head, Maggie was getting pretty hot. She didn't want to be drenched with sweat when she met with the elusive Mr. MacIntyre, and she did plan to meet him today. As for her clothes, if they were a little worse for wear, she reasoned calmly, it would merely add to her damsel-in-distress appearance. And she did so want to be rescued—from the loneliness of her life.

Her decision made, Maggie drew a bolstering breath. "Fine. But you scoot forward first."

Again, his brow lifted.

"You have more grease and dirt on the front of you than on the back. I don't want to ruin my clothes."

"Suit yourself." Looking as if he could care less either way, he gripped her hand. She put a foot in the stirrup, swung herself up onto his horse's back, and situated herself in the saddle, behind him. It was a tighter fit than she had imagined. Even with her hands out on either side of her for balance, her torso was snugly cossetted against the cowboy's back. She felt every rock-solid muscle in his shoulders, back, waist, hips and thighs. And more disturbing than his solid male strength was his sizzling warmth. Being pressed against him was like stretching out on sun-warmed concrete after a swim; Maggie immediately felt all warm inside.

If he felt a similar reaction, he did not show it. His manner brusque, he snapped, "Wrap your arms around my waist, unless you want to fall off."

Unable to see around the broadness of his shoulders, Maggie fumbled for something to hold on to, hitting his belt, her pinky grazing the top of his fly before she finally located the saddle horn and gripped it tightly. As the enormity of her error sunk in, she was glad he could not see her blush; her face must have been fire-engine red.

"Ready?" he drawled, the low husky timbre of his voice telling her he was as taken aback by her unwitting miscalculation as she was.

Maggie nodded, swallowing around the unaccustomed tightness in her throat. "The sooner we get there, the better," she said.

THEY RODE IN SILENCE until they reached the stables. Once there, Maggie was quick to dismount. J.D. followed. The middle of the day, the stables were empty, save for a few horses down at the opposite end of the building. Looking completely unaffected by their enforced closeness on the ride back, J.D. strode into the tack room. His purposeful footsteps echoing on the concrete stable floor, he returned with a small ferrier's box and knelt beside Buttercup. Picking up the horseshoe, he used a file to buff the tiny nick on the edge where it had been pulled off until it was smooth as silk.

"You're going to make the repair?" Maggie asked, not sure whether she was pleased or disappointed he was attending to her "problem with her horse" so quickly.

"I'm trained to do simple repairs. Does it bother you?"

"No, I'm grateful." She paused, knowing if she did not act quickly the opportunity she had sought would slip away from her. "Shouldn't we tell Mr. MacIntyre I'm here, though?" Maggie asked, edging slightly away from J.D.

He regarded her with an irreverent smile. "Not if you know what's good for you."

She watched him back, her gaze direct and cool. Something was going on here. Something more than he was willing to let on. "Why do I get the feeling you are trying to keep me from meeting your boss?" Even if it initially ticked off MacIntyre to find out she'd wandered accidentally-on-purpose onto his land, why should it matter to J.D. what happened to her? He didn't know her from Adam.

He ignored her question as he dropped his file in the toolbox, and brought out the appropriate size and numbers of nails with which to fasten the shoe onto Buttercup's foot. "If you're husband hunting, you're going to be disappointed," he warned, as if he could care less what she did. "Jake MacIntyre is not the marrying kind."

Those were famous last words, in Maggie's opinion. Anyone could get married. It just took meeting the right person at the right time, which was, coincidentally, exactly what she was prepared to do, for her and her Mr. Right.

"Nor is he the romantic fool you seem to expect him to be," J.D. continued speaking respectfully of the man who employed him as he picked out a farrier's hammer, too.

Maggie propped her hands on her slender hips. She couldn't say why exactly; she just knew something was up. "Why don't you let me be the judge of that?" she asked casually.

"Suit yourself." Laconically, J.D. put down his equipment and strode toward the phone on the stable wall. He picked it up and punched in three numbers, then waited, his sizzling dark brown eyes locked with Maggie's sky blue ones, until the person on the other end answered.

"Harry, it's me." J.D. rubbed the back of his neck in an irritated fashion. "I got this woman down here. Yeah, the trespasser." He paused to shoot Maggie a knowing look that made her flush. "She insists on meeting Jake personally. Yeah, I know. I told her he probably wouldn't cotton none to bein' interrupted in the middle of a workday, but she's insisting, and I don't think she's gonna leave—not voluntarily anyway—without..." He paused, as if interrupted by the person on the other end of the line.

Relaxing slightly, Maggie lounged against the post. Euphoria poured through her. She was about to get her wish. She was just that much closer to her goal.

"Yeah. Five minutes would be fine. Thanks, Harry." J.D. hung up the phone. Turning, he strode toward her, his strides long and lazy. "Uh...the boss'll be right down."

Maggie smiled, glad her plan was getting back on track once again, after the slight detour of running into J.D.

"See, that wasn't so hard, was it?" she asked.

Without warning, J.D. leaned impertinently close, one arm planted beside her, the other resting above her head. "Sure you don't want to reconsider?" he whispered in a low seductive voice that sent shivers down her spine.

"Reconsider what?" Maggie asked breathlessly, aware she couldn't move a centimeter without their bodies touching.

J.D. stroked a hand wantonly down the side of her face. "Going after something a little less rich."

Maggie jerked away from the disturbing warmth and sensuality of his touch.

"How do you know I want someone rich?"

"Honey, someone's going to have to bring in the dough to support you in the style to which you've been accustomed. And since you just quit your day job—"

"How do you know that?" Maggie demanded, outraged.

"How could I not?" he countered cooly, "When your every move is documented by the press. Not that everyone believes you're quitting modeling, though. Industry insiders claim you're just announcing this faux retirement as a publicity stunt designed to get you even more money the next time around."

Maggie scowled. "You are totally out of line."

"Like I said, honey, your picture and the sad story of your breakup with your ex-fiancé is in all the magazines." J.D. paused, repeating something else he had obviously heard. "Guess he wasn't rich enough for you, was he?"

Maggie would've liked to say the big discrepancy between her ex-fiancé's annual income and hers had nothing to do with their breakup, but that wasn't true.

The truth was money—or his lack of it—had everything to do with the demise of their relationship.

But, damn it, she was tired of the public speculation. "I'm not inclined to explain the intimate details of my private life to you or anyone else," she informed him.

His eyes darkened. "It annoys you that people think you're shallow," he guessed with mock sympathy.

Maggie tossed her head indignantly. "Of course it does."

He lifted his dark brows in a speculative manner. "So why not prove the gossips wrong then and go after someone a little less hard to get," he suggested in a low impertinent voice.

"Meaning you, I suppose?" Maggie countered, just as cooly.

"Why not?" he taunted, ever so softly, wrapping both arms about her sides and shoulders and gathering her close. "I may not be in the market for a wife, but I sure enjoy a toss in the hay every now and then."

Incensed, Maggie planted both hands on his chest and pushed with all her might, in the process gaining nary an inch of freedom. "You, sir, have gone too far," she told him, breasts heaving as she struggled to drag air into her lungs.

"Really?" J.D. lifted his brow. "The way I see it, I haven't gone nearly far enough." That said, he hauled her all the way into his arms and lowered his head ever so slowly, ever so deliberately to hers. Until his lips were close. "But I could," he murmured.

"No doubt," Maggie retorted, furious at the liberty he was taking. But that wasn't going to happen because she was not going to let herself get sidetracked into forgetting her dream. It was someone as rich and successful as she was that she had her sights on. Someone who would not use her or take advantage, she reminded herself stoically as he drew her closer yet and she drank in the scent and feel and strength of him. Her knees grew weak and spirals of desire swept through her in overwhelming waves.

And no matter how powerful the chemistry between them, she could not give in to it, or let the reckless, ill-mannered cowboy further it with the kiss he seemed dying to steal....

Breathing hard, she shoved away from him. Something she was able to do only because he loosened his possessive grip. As she stared up at him with a mixture of anger and confusion, she caught sight of the smug look on his face. Clearly, he thought he had won this brief battle of wills.

Deciding it was a mistake to let the rakish cowboy get away with anything, she lifted a hand and slapped him hard across the face. To her frustration, his expression altered only slightly.

Shocked by the ferocity of her feelings and the passionate nature of her behavior, she dropped her hand to her side. She'd had plenty of passes come her way—in her business it came with the territory—but she had never slapped anyone before, never mind with such unbridled force. What had gotten into her? What had gotten into him, or was he—the rascal—always this way? Was that why he was able to take her slap in stride?

Though his face had to be stinging unbearably, J.D. merely grinned and rubbed his jaw. "Like me that much, huh?" he drawled, the corners of his dark mustache quirking up.

"I like you that little," Maggie corrected hotly as footsteps sounded behind them. They turned in unison, and found themselves facing a slightly dour-looking barrel-chested man in an incredibly expensive double-breasted suit and tie. At a height of a little under five and a half feet, he barely came to Maggie's shoulder. Worse, he looked at least two decades older than either Maggie or J.D.

"J.D.!" the man demanded irately, looking first at Maggie, then at the arrogant hired hand with the red mark across his cheek. "Just what in blazes is going on here?"

# Chapter Two

"Sorry, boss," J.D. replied with a proper amount of chagrin. Looking not the least bit apologetic as he swung back around to face her, he locked eyes with Maggie again and slid a hand in the back pocket of his jeans. "Guess I got carried away."

"And then some," Maggie muttered, beneath her breath, so just J.D. could hear. But then, so had she, letting him hold her that close, even for a second! Darn it all, what had gotten into her? It was seeing that fortune-teller Sabrina again, hearing she was meant to marry a cowboy, that was predisposing her to all sorts of crazy things, Maggie reassured herself. Now that she was aware of it, she could and would curtail such behavior at once.

"Are you all right, miss?" J.D.'s boss asked.

"I'm fine." Maggie forced a smile, unable to completely contain her disappointment over the way things were turning out. "My horse was in trouble." She pointed to the palomino still standing calmly in the stable aisleway. "Buttercup threw a shoe."

"I see." The boss looked at Maggie's horse, then the ill-mannered cowboy in his employ. "J.D.—?" he began expectantly, in a tone that brooked no disobedience.

"I'll get Buttercup reshod in a hurry," J.D. promised.

His boss frowned and advised curtly, "See that you do. We would not want to delay Miss—?"

"Porter. Maggie Porter."

"—any longer than absolutely necessary." Jake MacIntyre's voice was heavy with meaning. He lowered his bifocals and looked down his nose at her. "I trust in the future you'll take pains to stay off the Rollicking M, as this is *private property.*" He stressed the last words to a censuring degree.

Maggie flushed with embarrassment over the many mistakes she had made since sauntering onto Rollicking M property, the least of which was passionately tangling with one of Jake MacIntyre's hired hands. She wished she had never come here. Never mind put one Jake MacIntyre at the top of her list of potential husbands.

She gathered her composure around her like a protective cloak. "No problem," she retorted breezily. "I apologize for any inconvenience I may have caused you." *I'm on to the next man on my list already.* To heck with what the fortune-teller Sabrina had said.

Nodding in satisfaction, assured that the situation had been resolved, J.D.'s boss left.

"I told you that you'd be disappointed," J.D. remarked, the moment they were alone again, as he swung around and surged toward her. "The boss is not exactly your type, is he?"

Boy, was that an understatement, Maggie thought, unable to help but be disappointed in a romantic sense by the man she had just met. Talk about a lack of chemistry! J.D.'s boss was stuffy, out of shape, over-dressed, and, judging by the ridiculous way he combed his hair to try to camouflage his bald spot, hopelessly out of touch with current thinking. Bald men were sexy: Sean Connery had proved as much.

Aware J.D. was waiting for an answer, Maggie shrugged. There had been no pictures of Jake Mac-Intyre in any of the articles she had read, as the reclusive millionaire did not like the Houston party scene. And she couldn't find one person to share any details about the man. "I just figured your boss would be different, that's all."

J.D. lifted a curious brow. "Different," he drawled in a low jealous tone. "How so?"

Maggie hesitated, not sure whether to answer or not. Then, figuring it didn't matter since she was leaving the Rollicking M anyway, she forced herself to answer confidentially, "From what I know about Jake Mac-Intyre—"

"Which is—?" J.D. asked impatiently, dark eyes blazing.

Maggie drew on her research. "He inherited this ranch from his father and spent the last fifteen years or so building the Rollicking M into one of the best-run ranches in Texas."

J.D. shrugged, clearly unimpressed. "A lot of people have made more of ranches than their folks."

"True," Maggie agreed, leaning against the post, "but not many also have a chain of Houston busi-nesses that make them a millionaire several times over. Nor do they have reputations for donating so generously and continuously to local hospitals and children's charities.''

J.D. folded his arms across his chest. ''You have done your homework, haven't you?''

Maggie tore her eyes from the bunched muscles of his biceps.

''Enough to know that your boss is a determined bachelor who avoids the party circuit like the plague and allegedly pays a public relations firm to keep his photos, what few there are of him, out of the press.''

''Jake MacIntyre likes his privacy.''

''Apparently.''

Half J.D.'s mouth curved into a taunting grin. His teeth flashed white against his sable brown mustache. ''You thought he'd be handsome, didn't you?''

''More rugged, actually.'' *Ruggedly handsome.* She shook her head in wonderment. ''For goodness sake, he's a rancher and he doesn't even have a suntan!'' Since when was that the norm?

''Tending to business keeps the boss indoors a lot,'' J.D. explained.

Maybe so. Still... The paleness of his boss's skin seemed a little peculiar to Maggie. ''What about the ranch?'' she asked resolutely. ''Doesn't that take him out in the sun?''

J.D. picked up the newly buffed and smoothed horseshoe, he fitted it against Buttercup's foot and nailed it on. ''He leaves the running of the ranch to me, which as it happens, is the way I like it.''

Maggie stroked Buttercup's mane to keep her calm. ''So you're the boss around here?'' J.D. was so difficult to deal with, she found that hard to believe.

He nodded at her affirmatively as he finished nailing

the shoe and studied his handiwork, finding it satisfactory. "Most of the time, I'm the one here telling them what to do."

"Hmm." Maggie watched Buttercup test out the newly refitted shoe.

"What's that 'hmm' supposed to mean?"

"Nothing." Satisfied Buttercup was okay, Maggie let go of her mare's halter and turned back to J.D. "Just hmm."

Silence fell between them as they sized each other up. J.D. closed his farrier's toolbox and carried it back to the tack room. "Figure out you've wasted your time here yet?" he said over his shoulder as he washed his hands.

Maggie joined him at the rough metal sink as she washed her hands, too. "Any time you learn something it is never a waste of time."

And this afternoon she had learned a lot, she thought as they reached for the paper towels at the same time. For starters, her foolproof plan to find a mate might look good on paper, but the reality was it had more holes than Swiss cheese. She'd gone to far too much trouble just to meet someone who wasn't even her type.

"But you're right," she continued, as they left the tack room with her in the lead. She started toward Buttercup. "I should be going."

He reached out and grabbed her wrist. "Not so fast."

She whirled to face him, anger sizzling in her sky blue eyes. He felt her stiffen beneath his touch. "Now what?" she demanded, jerking her gaze away from his.

He regarded her with unveiled amusement, even as he maintained his light, easy grip on her wrist. "How about a date?" His hand slid lower, to twine playfully with her palm.

She blinked, for a moment going very still. "Excuse me?"

J.D. grinned at the way she was suddenly trembling. Not with fear, he decided, but reaction to his nearness and the chemistry sizzling between them. "You know. A date. It's a social engagement or appointment arranged beforehand. In this case, between you and me."

Her mouth fell open in surprise, then just as swiftly snapped shut. "No."

The quick turndown both irked and amazed him. After all, he had felt the sweet yielding of her body against his. More than anything, he wanted her in his arms again. He sensed, though he figured she would be the last person on earth to admit it, that it was what she wanted, too.

"No?" he prodded.

Maggie dismissed him with a cool, haughty look that would have discouraged a lesser man. She jerked her hand from his. "Sorry. You're not my type."

He hooked his thumbs in the belt loops on either side of his fly and regarded her with a speculation he was sure she would just as soon avoid. "Funny, from the way you were looking at me a couple of minutes ago," he drawled, letting his eyes linger on the honeyed softness of her golden hair and the perfection of her ivory skin before returning to her long lashes and blue eyes, "I thought I was exactly your type."

"Well, you're wrong!" Maggie fumed, beginning

to look both nervous and embarrassed as she stepped back swiftly and came up against a post.

He watched deep pink color sweep across her face as he once again slowly, deliberately closed the distance between them. "What's the matter, princess, am I not rich enough for your blood?"

Maggie swept off her hat and raked a hand through her hair, pushing it off her face. "Money has nothing to do with it."

Hearing her fib sent anger surging through him all over again; if there was one thing he wanted from the women tromping through this ranch on a weekly basis, it was honesty. "Bull! Money has everything to do with it. That and the fact you're after the owner of the ranch." He planted a hand on either side of her, trapping her against the post. "Providing he's handsome and sexy and not a simple ranch hand."

"You're a ranch hand and there's nothing simple about you, J.D.," Maggie told him dryly, letting her hat drop to her side.

"True." He was glad she had noticed. "So you'll give up on the boss and go out with me?"

"Sorry." Maggie dismissed his suggestion with a repressive glance and an uncaring wave of her hat in his direction. "I don't need any reminders of my fiasco here."

Like hell she didn't, J.D. thought.

"Not even this?" he asked as he quickly, expertly hauled her back into his arms, lowered his head to hers, and throwing caution to the wind, stole a quick but thorough kiss. At the touch of their lips, she melted in his arms, just the way he'd thought she would.

The bittersweet pangs of desire, the yearning to be

close to someone again, both so long absent from his life, came flooding back with gargantuan force. How long, he wondered as he tangled his hands in the soft fullness of her golden hair, since he'd been presented with such a challenge, or been near a woman he'd wanted even half as much? How long since he'd ached with pleasure and been more drawn to the present than the past?

Maggie didn't know how it had happened. She had plotted the day's events so carefully! But somehow, she had lost the upper hand. Her carefully orchestrated husband hunt had been sidetracked by a reckless cowboy who thought nothing of hauling her into his strong arms, pressing her against his hard, muscled length, and kissing her as if there were no tomorrow for either of them, only today. And as his hot, clever lips wrenched an unwilling response from her, she began to feel as if there were only this moment, this man. His thick mustache tickled her upper lip and his unshaven jaw scorched the tender skin of her face. But she knew she had no choice but to put the boundaries back.

Maggie drew herself up with a low moan of regret, and pushed him away.

SILENCE STRETCHED between them, broken only by the uneven rasp of their breaths. It didn't take a genius, J.D. noted, to see that Maggie regretted the kiss ever happening. Maggie squared her shoulders and gave him a withering look as she replaced her hat squarely on her head. "You need to go somewhere and cool off. Now."

J.D. grinned, thinking the best way to do that would

be to make long, luxurious love with her, in places
both hot and cool. He tipped the brim of his hat back,
to better see her face, and widened his eyes appreciatively. "I'm willing, if you are."

She moistened her lips and gave him a droll look
as she tugged the brim of her hat lower across her
honey blond brow. "I imagine you've heard this before, cowboy, but you are much too forward for your
own good," she told him passionately.

He knew. "That's 'cause I realize life is too short
for me not to go after what I want, when I want it,
and what I want right now is you, Maggie Porter," he
said softly, pushing aside the bittersweet memories of
his own loss, and using the direct, honest approach
that had always worked for him in the past.

But it didn't work on Maggie.

Her sassy chin lifted. Her eyes, serious and determined now, met his.

"Well that's just too bad," she retorted. "Because
what I want is a husband, *not* a hot-blooded lover."

J.D. eyed her unhappily as he forgot about his own
problems and started concentrating on her. He'd
thought the worst of her from the get-go and, damn it,
it was all true. All she cared about was snagging herself a rich hubby. "That why you pulled your horse's
shoe off after you ignored all the No Trespassing signs
and wandered onto the ranch?" he demanded.

Maggie regarded him with a stunned look. "How
did you know about that?" she asked incredulously.

J.D. shrugged and rocked his weight forward onto
the balls of his feet. "There are hidden security cam-
eras all over the ranch, to protect against just such
intrusions." He narrowed his glance at her. "Seems

there are a lot of women these days who are determined to marry millionaire ranchers. That was the plan, wasn't it? Play the damsel in distress and hope your plight would be brought directly to Jake MacIntyre's attention?" He gave her a look that dared her to admit it.

Maggie stiffened rebelliously under his bluntly assessing gaze. "I admit I've researched suitable mates," she replied recalcitrantly as she folded her arms tightly beneath her breasts. "Jake MacIntyre just happened to be first on my list."

"That's the most cockeyed plan I've ever heard," Jake said, tearing his eyes from the soft, womanly curves of her breasts, and returning his attention to her upturned face.

"I disagree," Maggie said with a stubbornness that would have been winning if it were not so ill-advised. "I think it's bound to work better than anything else I have done."

J.D. leaned in close enough to pick up the intoxicating fragrance of her perfume. "Which is what exactly?" he asked, as the fragrance of her set off a chain reaction within him that went straight to his groin.

"Wait for the right man to come along and sweep me off my feet."

J.D. didn't know why exactly—things like this generally didn't bother him, hadn't for a long while—but he didn't want to think about Maggie with another man. Particularly one who was not suited for her and vice versa. "It hasn't happened?" he ascertained.

Once she had come close, Maggie remembered, only to find out all was not as it seemed. She shook her head sadly. "Not by a long shot. But that's all

right. It will happen,'' she said, determined. ''I just
need to keep looking.''

''There are more efficient ways of looking.'' J.D.
promised as he leaned in as if to kiss her again.

Her heart racing, Maggie braced her hand on his
chest and held him at bay. ''As I said, I am looking
for the marrying kind, cowboy.'' She studied him
cooly. ''Something tells me you are not that.''

He reacted as if it amazed him to discover how
close she was to the truth. He stepped back, much to
her dismay.

''I admit marriage is not what I'm looking for,'' he
said, as he led her horse back out into the sunshine.

''Just as I figured,'' Maggie said, disappointed despite herself. Which was too bad. For one crazy reckless second, she had been tempted to give in to temp-
tation and go on a date with him. Why, she didn't
know. ''See you, then.'' She grabbed Buttercup's reins
and prepared to remount.

Before she could swing herself up into the saddle,
a stern woman in a starched white nurse's uniform
charged into the courtyard between the stables and the
ranch house. She was dragging two squirming mud-
covered pint-sized little boys by their shirt collars. She
looked ready to deliver the spanking of a lifetime. And
the little prekindergartners knew it.

''Save us, Unka Jake! Save us before she whales
the tar out of us!'' they shouted, looking straight at
J.D.

''Uncle Jake?'' Maggie repeated, dumbfounded.
Jake wasn't here. She narrowed her glance at J.D. Or
was he?

Frowning, the cowboy who'd introduced himself as

J.D. reached to rescue the two wildly squirming boys. As the nurse let go of them, they sagged against J.D. in silent, mortified relief, and held on tight.

"What the devil is going on here?" J.D. demanded.

"I'll tell you what's going on here," the nurse announced, looking straight at J.D. "I've had it with these two ruffians. Mr. MacIntyre, I quit!"

# Chapter Three

Maggie turned to J.D. alias Jake MacIntyre. "You rotten scheming lowlife!"

The real Jake MacIntyre grinned at her, even as he struggled to hold on to his two squirming nephews. "Isn't that a little like the pot calling the kettle black?" he inquired with a taunting grin.

Aware she had never felt more humiliated or embarrassed in her life, Maggie fumed, "You deliberately misrepresented yourself to me!"

"Hey," he said with mock defensiveness, "a lot of my friends do call me J.D. At least they did when I was growing up."

"But you couldn't resist tweaking me just a little," Maggie asserted, thoroughly incensed, yet spellbound just the same. Darn it all, she wished his mesmerizing chocolate brown eyes weren't so full of mischief and that his dark mustache didn't curl up so roguishly at the corners when he smiled.

Jake shrugged. "When I heard you were coming—"

"Really." Maggie lifted a brow. "How?"

Clearly, Jake thought, she did not believe he'd been tipped off.

Jake grinned, leaned a little closer, and enlightened her smugly. "A friend at the *Houston Chronicle* told me—"

"What exactly?" Maggie interrupted again, looking a little less sure of herself.

"—that you were doing research on a number of rich, eligible Texans. And that, of all of them, I interested you the most. Seein' as how I don't appreciate bein' spied on or wanted for my money, I figured I'd have a little fun with you when you did show up. And now that I've done so, I figure we're even."

"Not quite," Maggie replied, still fuming as she planted her hands on her slender hips. "But we will be," she promised hotly. One way or another, Jake MacIntyre would rue the day he had laid eyes on her.

Jake looked down at his nephews—to see them still staring, enthralled, at their visitor—before he shot Maggie a wicked grin. "I look forward to it," he drawled. "Now, Nurse Ratchet—" Jake turned his attention to the furious woman in white. "How about a raise—effective immediately—and a promise that my nephews will be good from here on out."

"Your nephews couldn't be good if they tried, which they certainly are not doing!" Nurse Ratchet replied, her patience with all the MacIntyre men obviously exhausted. "And furthermore, my name is not Nurse Ratchet—"

"Coulda fooled me," Jake muttered beneath his breath.

Amused, it was all Maggie could do not to grin.

"I am leaving as soon as I collect my two weeks'

severance pay from Harry Wholesome. And good rid-
dance, I say!'' Turning on her heel, the nurse marched
away. Behind her, Jake's two nephews stuck out their
tongues at her departing backside.

"Hey.'' Jake frowned at them. "Cut that out.'' His
frown deepened. "It's not polite.''

"Sorry,'' the one with the red hair and freckles finally said.

"But she's not nice,'' his towheaded brother explained.

"Not at all.''

And then questions came all at once.

"Unka Jake, who is this lady?''

"She's pretty.''

"Is she your girlfriend?''

"Not yet,'' Jake boasted with a devil-may-care grin
aimed in Maggie's direction. "But she will be,'' he
vowed.

"Ha! In your dreams, cowboy,'' Maggie told him.

And was rewarded with a dazzling smile from Jake.

"Fellas,'' Jake said with much too much flamboy-
ance. "I'd like you to meet Maggie Porter. She's been
trespassing on the ranch, but because she's such a
great kisser,'' he stated magnanimously, "I've decided
to forgive her.''

Astounded by his brazen account of the situation—
she'd met a lot of rogues in her time but Jake took the
prize!—Maggie blushed before she gasped.

"You been kissing her, already?'' one of the little
boys asked, amazed, and more than a little impressed.

"Sure have, and I'd like to do so again, too,'' Jake
admitted recklessly, tossing yet another grin in Maggie's direction. "Soon as I finish introducing you-all,

that is. Maggie, this freckled-face rodeoer is Rusty—named such 'cause of all his red hair. He looks like his daddy. His younger brother here, the towheaded one who looks like his Mama, is Wyatt. As you may or may not have guessed, they are fraternal twins, and they are four and a half years old. Guys, shake hands with the lady.'' Grinning as widely as their bad-boy uncle, the two boys promptly held out mud-drenched hands. ''Well, maybe not,'' Jake said hastily, cutting off the cordial greetings until further notice. ''Leastwise, 'til the two of you get washed up.''

''Aw, do we have to?'' Rusty complained, with a pout.

''We was just gettin' to the good part,'' Wyatt added, looking as downtrodden by the denial. ''You know, where the mud's all squishy and just right.''

''That's when ol' Nurse Ratchet came out, and made us stop,'' Rusty confided in a voice barely above a stage whisper.

''Tried to,'' Wyatt corrected, determined to get the recitation of facts right. ''We didn't stop, least not 'til she grabbed us by our ears. Then, of course, we had to stop,'' he explained solemnly.

''But can we go back to it?'' Rusty asked Jake, wide-eyed, obviously hoping that their roughhousing and misbehaving was not over yet.

His manner turning abruptly solemn and parental, Jake shook his head firmly. ''No. I think you boys have had enough fun in the mud for one day. It's time to get cleaned up. Though how we're gonna do it, is a good question.'' Jake smoothed his thick, sable brown mustache with the ends of his suntanned fingers as he studied his nephews, perplexed. ''If I take you on back to the ranch house like this, Harry is going to have a fit. And you know, considering all the mud you'd be likely to track into the ranch house in that condition, I can't say as I'd blame him.''

"Harry Wholesome?" Maggie interjected, intrigued by the domestic drama despite herself. Whether he wanted to own up to it or not, Jake MacIntyre did have a serious, responsible side.

"Yeah," Jake replied. "You met him a few minutes ago."

Maggie blinked. "The 'boss man'?"

"Yep, that's Harry Wholesome," Jake affirmed.

"And Harry does not like messes," Rusty piped up.

Wyatt nodded solemnly as he shook his head in obvious warning. "Nobody better track mud on his clean floors, let me tell you."

Maggie grinned.

Jake was still studying his two nephews, who were coated with grime from head to toe. Finally, he stopped stroking his mustache, dropped his hand to his side, and said, "Maybe the best thing to do is wash you off with the hose out back. Then let you go swimming in the pool. And then take you in the house, and put you in the shower."

"That ought do it," Rusty said, echoing Maggie's thoughts exactly.

"Let's go," Wyatt hollered.

Jake put up a staying hand, stopping them before they even got started. "Hold on a minute, fellas." Jake looked at Maggie. Taking her by the arm, Jake drew her slightly aside. "Want to help?" he asked, fastening his eyes on hers.

Maggie laughed, his invitation was so outrageous.

After the way he'd treated her! "Why would I want to do you any favors?" she prodded, loathe to admit that despite everything she was tempted. His nephews were so cute. Their presence so lively and entertaining. This familiar energy and activity was exactly what had been missing from her life.

"Because I'm clearly in over my head here?" Jake guessed.

Maggie folded her arms in front of her stoically. "Try again," she dared, letting him know with one raking glance he was not likely to win.

"So I won't have you—" Jake put his fist against lips and coughed "—arrested—" he coughed again "—for trespassing? Now wouldn't that be a story for the *Houston Chronicle,*" he mused, his dark-lashed eyes brimming over with mischief once again. "Supermodel returns to Texas in search for rich hubby. Why, people would eat that up!"

"I bet they would," Maggie drawled. "That's not, however, the kind of local news I intended on making."

Jake nodded solemnly. "Bet you figured on a big wedding announcement in the paper instead. A picture of you all gussied up in your wedding finery."

"Not just me. The man of my dreams would be in the paper, too. In the engagement photo."

Jake smiled at her smugly. "Sounds like you got it all worked out. I'd sure hate to have to put a monkey wrench in your plans, particularly since you're such a famous person and all."

That kind of deleterious publicity she did not need, particularly since she was determined to continue her husband hunt until she found and married a candidate aeons more suitable than good ol' Jake. "I thought you liked your privacy," Maggie interrupted, not about to tell him he had quickly regained the upper hand in their standoff of wills, even though he had.

"Yeah." Jake grinned, readily admitting this was so. "But I like seeing you squirm more," he replied, rubbing his jaw with his index finger.

Maggie could believe this was so.

"So what's it going to be?" Jake asked, dropping his hand to his side. He regarded her wilfully. "You gonna help me or not?"

ONE GOOD TURN did deserve another, Maggie thought, and Jake had helped her reshoe Buttercup. Plus, the inherent mischievousness of his nephews reminded her a lot of her three younger brothers, when they had been growing up. The fact Jake was successfully blackmailing her with bad publicity and could ruin her plans to quickly and efficiently find a husband and by extension, family, for herself had nothing to do with her change of heart, she assured herself sternly.

Maggie removed her flat-brimmed hat. She slapped it against one jean-clad thigh. "Considering your nurse just quit, I suppose I could stay long enough to see that Rusty and Wyatt are okay," Maggie conceded reluctantly after a moment.

Jake grinned. "But don't read anything into it," Maggie warned as the four of them left the barn in tandem and headed for the rear of the ranch house at a leisurely pace.

"No, ma'am, I sure won't," Jake drawled, letting her know that he did.

Maggie merely rolled her eyes in exasperation. She

was not falling for this cowboy's tricks! Moving forward, she took Rusty and Wyatt by their grimy little hands. Ignoring Jake, she said, "So, you guys are pretty quick, right?"

They nodded in the affirmative. "We sure are," Wyatt bragged, carefully adapting the confident male swagger of his uncle Jake.

"How long do you reckon it's going to take for us to get you cleaned up enough for a swim in the pool?" Maggie asked, well aware Jake was not only letting her take charge of the situation, but falling slightly behind them. In fact, she could feel his heated gaze lovingly caressing her shoulders, hips, thighs...

"Ten minutes," Wyatt guessed.

"Five," Rusty disagreed.

Maggie turned to Jake and found his eyes roving her face. She regarded him with defiance. She didn't care what he thought. No matter what he had on her, he was not going to get the better of her. "You got some suits for these boys?"

The intense male interest in his gaze stripped away the apathy that had been so much a part of her life since her engagement had ended. All at once, she felt thoroughly alive, challenged. Like the possibilities for happiness were endless. "They're in the cabana, next to the pool," he replied.

She tore her eyes from his mocking half smile. "Then I'll let you be in charge of the changing while I take care of rinsing them off."

"I CAN'T BELIEVE you hosed them down and got them changed in less than ten minutes," Jake said, as his two nephews jumped into the shallow end of the pool and began swimming and playing energetically. Reduced to the role of spectator by her take-charge manner, he moved beneath the shade of the patio umbrella and dropped into a comfortable white deck chair.

"It's simple." Maggie took a sip of her iced tea and set it on the table between she and Jake. "You just have to get them interested in cooperating first."

"How'd you do that?" Jake poured himself a glass of iced tea.

"Charm. You ought to try it sometime."

Jake merely grinned at her and continued sipping his iced tea.

"How long are you in charge of your nephews?" Maggie asked.

"It's hard to say," he admitted with a concerned tone.

Maggie lifted a brow, curious.

Jake continued reluctantly, in a low voice only Maggie could hear, "My sister, Kelsey, the boys' mother, is in the midst of a personal crisis. She asked me to take care of them for a few days."

Judging from the look on Jake's face, it was some crisis. "How long have they been here?" Maggie asked.

"Two weeks, so far."

"That must be hard on the boys." Maggie couldn't help notice Rusty and Wyatt as they slanted sly looks at Jake and surreptitiously edged—or so they clearly thought—toward the deep end of the pool.

"It has been and is," Jake confirmed, still keeping an eye on his nephews. When they continued on their path, he stood and waved the two imps toward the shallow end. "Guys, you know the rule. I don't care how well you learned to swim this summer. You can't be in the water over your head unless an adult is in the pool with you." He waited until they had headed toward the shallow end before he continued, "They've never been without their mom for this long. I think that's one of the reasons they've been giving all the nurses such heck."

"*All* the nurses?" Maggie queried bluntly. Exactly what was going on here?

"Nurse Ratchet was number five," Jake told her, chagrined. He shoved a hand through the wind-tossed layers of his sable brown hair. "I don't think I can get another one out here."

"Maybe you should look for a governess instead," Maggie suggested, taking another sip of tea.

"My thoughts exactly," Jake agreed. He looked at her as if drawn to her in a way he hadn't thought possible. "So, are you interested in the job—for more than ten minutes?" he asked casually.

Maggie blinked. She had started out here as an annoyingly forward trespasser in his view. Or had he forgotten? "You're kidding, right?" she drawled, wondering what he was up to now.

But Jake only shook his head and slapped the brim of his Stetson against his muscular jean-clad knee. "I wish to heck I was." He nodded at the pool. "You can see for yourself what a handful these two little fellas are. Harry can't handle them and I still have a ranch and numerous businesses to run."

Maggie shrugged. "So take a few days off," she advised, giving him a long steady look that let him know she accepted no excuses for deliberately letting someone down. She knew all the reasons why people shirked their duty to the family, and firsthand how much sacrifice it took to personally fulfil them. She also knew it was worth it, in the end, knowing you'd helped your family in every way you possibly could.

"I've already done that, between nurses." Jake paused. He leaned closer, his voice low. And sexy, in a disturbingly sensual way. "I'd pay you well," he promised softly, "if that's what's worrying you."

Maggie stiffened as she kept her eyes on his nephews, as they paddled and splashed about. "I can just imagine the fringe benefits you have in mind." She refused to meet the suggestive promise in his eyes.

Jake grinned and stroked the ends of his mustache in a way that let her know he did indeed have loving her on his mind.

"But I am no governess," Maggie continued.

"Ah, but you do know how to handle little boys."

"I should. I reared my three brothers."

"Really?"

"Yes, though from a much older age."

"Great. I knew there was a reason I thought you were perfect."

Judging by the heat of his gaze, Maggie was not so sure that was it.

"And as you can see," he concluded in a hurry, clearly anxious to wrap up this deal, "I'm desperate, so name your price."

Maggie swiveled toward him, so their knees collided, and set him straight. "It's not money I'm interested in, Jake."

"Then what?" He made no move to draw away from her.

Determined to show him she was no cowering

schoolgirl but a self-made woman who could meet him on equal terms, she made no move to draw away, either. "I want a husband and a family of my own."

This information neither pleased nor surprised Jake, she noted.

"But he has to be rich," Jake ascertained, some of the light going out of his dark brown eyes.

"For a lot of reasons," Maggie conceded cautiously, determined to be perfectly truthful in her dealings with Jake and any other man, "yes, he does."

Jake was silent a long moment, thinking and weighing the situation, she guessed, just as she had. Finally, he gave an indifferent shrug she was not sure she entirely believed.

"Well, then, I'll help you find that rich husband you are looking for, if you'll help me out meantime," he said.

"How will you help me?" Maggie queried, fearing there was a catch to this newfound cooperation from him.

"I'll introduce you around, personally. After all, I know a lot of rich ranchers and businessmen," he said.

Maggie paused, studying the ruggedly handsome contours of his face. "You'd do this for me, knowing that I want to snare one of them?" She focused on the golden hue of his suntanned skin.

"Sure, I will," Jake promised with an easy grin and a subtly taunting sheen in his eyes. "I'll just preface the introduction with the fact you're on the lookout for a rich husband." His sexy smile deepened. "Forewarned is forearmed, in my opinion."

"So is she gonna stay and baby-sit us, Unka Jake?" Rusty yelled from the pool.

"They know what we're discussing?" Maggie interrupted in astonishment, not sure how she felt about that, except maybe pressured. She did not want to let the cute little boys down.

"I told 'em I'd ask you, when they were changing into their swimsuits," Jake replied. He looked at his nephews and held out both palms in a gesture that said it could still go either way. "Don't know yet," he shouted.

"How come?" Wyatt yelled, looking perplexed.

"She's not convinced we need her yet," Jake replied loudly. He turned to Maggie and locked eyes with her deliberately. Ever so sexily, he added in a low voice that said he did indeed have bedrooms and long, hot, Texas nights on his mind, "But you-all will be glad to know I'm working on that..."

"I can see that you are."

Silence fell between them.

The boys looked at Maggie and Jake. They said something to each other. Then began to play again, diving down for colorful weighted swim rings.

Still sipping her iced tea, Maggie watched as Rusty dove after a swim ring. Seconds passed. When he did not immediately surface in the shallow end, she stood to see what he was doing. So did Jake. Rusty wasn't in the shallow end, as he was supposed to be, he had covered the length of the pool in one long breath and was swimming toward the deep end.

"Rusty, get back up here!" Jake commanded loudly.

"I'll get him, Unka Jake!"

"No, Wyatt," Jake said.

Too late. Holding his nose closed with two fingers,

Wyatt dove down after his brother. He tapped Rusty on the shoulder; both kicked their feet and shot upward. Maggie and Jake both simultaneously sighed their relief as the two boys broke through the surface of the water. Their relief was shortlived as Wyatt, abruptly struggling and looking as though he was suffering a major cramp, went under again.

"Help!" Rusty yelled frantically as he too began to panic and thrash about. "Unka Jake, Maggie, help!" He went under, too.

"Oh, my God," Maggie breathed, already kicking off her boots, right alongside Jake. "You get one, I'll get the other." Together, knowing there was no time to waste, they both jumped fully clothed into the deep end of the swimming pool.

As Maggie and Jake hit bottom, a safe distance from the boys and each other, the boys rocketed to the surface. By the time she and Jake came up for air, Wyatt and Rusty were both treading water with ease. It was easy to see that whatever had been going on, they had not been and were not now drowning. Maggie was immediately very relieved and very furious. And so was their uncle Jake.

"The shallow end! Now!" Jake ordered sternly.

The boys exchanged apprehensive looks. Heads down, they headed for the other end of the pool, swimming obediently, not stopping until they reached the other end. Jake followed, swimming with smooth purposeful strokes, as did Maggie. "What the heck do you guys think you were doing?" he demanded of his nephews as soon as he'd set them both up on the side of the pool, so they were sitting on the edge, their legs dangling in the water, from the calf down.

"We were just playing," Rusty defended himself, slicking his wet red hair away from his face.

"Yeah, we didn't mean to make you mad," Wyatt added, slicking his hair back, too, and looking as if he thought that should be the end of it.

"Well, I am mad," Jake shouted emotionally, not about to let his reckless nephews off so easily. "You two scared me to death! I thought you were drowning! Maggie and I both did!"

"Are you mad at us, too, Maggie?" Rusty asked, narrowing his eyes at her.

"I'm not mad," Maggie said calmly. *I almost had a heart attack but I am not mad.* "And neither is your uncle Jake. We just don't like being scared, that's all. And you guys really, really scared us," Maggie told them both emphatically.

"You have to quit clowning around like that," Jake said sternly as he surged out of the pool, stalked to the table and handed the boys each a thick beach towel. "Or else sometime you might really be in trouble and people'll just think you're goofing around again and no one will even try to help until it's too late."

"Kind of like the little boy who cried wolf in that story," Rusty explained, quite unnecessarily it seemed to his brother.

"Right," Jake said.

"Okay," Wyatt said cheerfully.

"Yeah," Rusty added, looking equally happy and trouble free, despite the scolding. "We won't do it again. We promise."

"I DIDN'T GET THROUGH to them, did I?" Jake said, after he'd sent the boys into the house to put on dry clothes.

"Judging by the happy looks on their faces just now," Maggie drawled as she accepted his helping hand out of the swimming pool, and pulled her damp clinging clothes away from the defining outline of her breasts, "I don't think so, no." Aware her nipples were contracting in the cooler air, she wrapped the towel he gave her around her shoulders and concentrated on the problem at hand. "Is this the first prank they've pulled?" she asked, a little breathlessly.

Jake tore his eyes from her soaked clothing, and all it revealed. "I wish."

Aware she was dripping water everywhere, Maggie sank into a deck chair. "You're worried about them?"

"Very much so." Jake rubbed a towel over his face and hair. Then sat too, and stripped off his socks. "It's not really that they're bad," he said as he began to unbutton his sodden shirt, "just that they need constant watching and looking after. I don't know," he mused in a low, troubled voice, opening his shirt and peeling it off, to reveal a tanned muscular chest with a mat of dark hair that was reminiscent of Tom Selleck in his Magnum P.I. days. "Maybe it is just the age. Maybe it's the fact that they're still a little upset by all the turmoil in their family and are acting out their unhappiness about it, but I can't believe how much trouble they can get into in so little time."

Maggie paused. With effort she tore her eyes from the magnificence of Jake's chest, and the long, muscular legs beneath his clinging jeans.

She could leave Jake. After all, he was very much capable of taking care of himself. The two little boys were something else.

"I'll stay and help you out, but only for a couple of days," she said, qualifying her response and worrying even as she did so that she was making a mistake by getting further involved with the swaggering cowboy, even for a little while. "And only until you find someone else."

# Chapter Four

"You're really going to take me up on my offer?" Jake said, looking amazed.

Maggie lifted the edge of her towel from her slender shoulder and delicately blotted her face. "I've never been able to turn my back on a child in need, and those two nephews of yours need to be closely watched if they are going to stay out of trouble." As she studied him briefly, she raked her teeth across the pouty softness of her lower lip. "Meantime, I expect you to hold up your end of the bargain," she admonished.

"No problem," Jake said easily, already regretting the hasty pledge he had made. "I'll help you find the husband of your dreams." Though why he was doing this, he didn't know. "But first, I have a couple of questions of my own."

"Such as?"

Jake let his gaze rove the water-dampened strands of her long golden blond hair. Her peaches-and-cream complexion was flawless in the brilliant September sunlight. "A beautiful woman like you, who's modeled all over the world... How come you haven't married before?'' He paused, awaiting her reply, even as he saw her blush slightly and hesitate. ''Or have you?''

''I haven't,'' Maggie replied quickly, turning her glance away, to the shimmering blue of the boot-shaped swimming pool.

He wanted her full attention—badly. Jake narrowed his eyes at her. ''You've been asked before,'' he said, astonished that no one had won this beauty's hand in marriage.

Maggie turned to him, composed now. And slightly aloof. ''More than once, in dozens of ways,'' she affirmed, as casually as if that happened to every woman every day.

''But you weren't serious,'' Jake guessed.

Maggie's mood turned visibly sad and reflective as she knotted her hands together and recalled, ''Once, I was.''

And yet she hadn't married, Jake surmised. He was very curious, unusually so. Jake asked bluntly, ''What happened?''

Maggie shrugged, the sad look remaining on her face. ''Three days before the wedding, I found out my fiancé didn't want to get married after all.'' She took a deep breath and sighed. ''He was just getting married to please me.'' The barest hint of hurt and depression colored her low tone. ''I didn't like feeling that way, like marriage to me was something my future husband felt he *had* to do, not something he *wanted* to do. So I broke it off and I promised myself that I would never marry anyone who didn't want to get married as much as I did,'' she finished matter-of-factly, having composed herself again.

"Good plan," Jake said, meaning it.

Looking as if her hopes were pinned firmly on her future, Maggie asked, "So, when do I meet my first Mr. Right?"

Jake thought a moment. There was no time like the present to show Maggie there were other paths to take, ones much more likely to grant her happiness, at least temporarily.

As for the future, well, no one knew better than he that tomorrow was nothing that could be counted on. The present was the only sure thing.

"How about tonight?" he suggested amiably.

"Is it true, Maggie?" Rusty asked earnestly, several hours later, as Maggie tucked the boys in their twin beds. "Do you really have a date tonight?"

"It's not really a date, more like an introduction," Maggie said as she scooped up miniature toy cars, stuffed animals and building blocks and tossed them willy-nilly into the brimming toy boxes at the foot of each bed.

A curious look on his face, Wyatt propped himself up on his elbow. Freshly scrubbed and clad in Texas Rangers pajamas, he looked cute enough to grace a children's clothing ad. And so did his fraternal twin brother. "So, when's he coming to see you?" Wyatt asked.

Maggie glanced at her watch, keeping track of the time. "Nine o'clock. Your uncle Jake invited him for a drink, but he said he doubted Mr. Benefield could stay long." Unable to trust Jake's newfound cooperativeness, Maggie paused. She knew the boys, at least, would be forthright with her. "Do you boys know Mr. Benefield?" she asked.

They solemnly shook their heads.

So much for finding out what her blind da—intro-duction would be like that way, Maggie thought, disappointed.

"What happens if you like Mr. Benefield?" Rusty asked uncertainly as he propped himself up on his elbow.

Maggie shrugged. "If I'm lucky we'll go out on a date sometime."

"Instead of Unka Jake?" Wyatt asked, frowning.

"Instead of Uncle Jake," Maggie confirmed, knowing that turn of events could only be good for her, as she already found bad-boy Jake MacIntyre far too sexy as it was. "Now, do you boys have everything you need?" Maggie asked, as she finished tidying their room for the night. They'd already had their bedtime snack, as well as a last trip to the bathroom.

"We're okay." Exhausted and yawning, both boys lay their heads on their pillows and snuggled beneath their covers.

"Now remember what I told you," Maggie schooled the boys firmly. "If you two are good for me, and go right to sleep tonight, we'll do something really special together tomorrow morning."

"'Kay, Maggie," Rusty said, seemingly pleased with the thought of that possibility. "We'll behave, we promise," he said.

"Good." Maggie smiled at both boys affectionately. "'Cause I'm counting on you two."

"We sure are glad you showed up," Wyatt told her, as she bent to say good-night and tuck him in. He gave her a hug. "'Cause me and Rusty—" Wyatt's voice caught as he unwound his small arms from around her neck "—we been awful sad."

The catch in his voice brought tears to Maggie's eyes; she never had been able to turn away from a child in need. She also knew what it felt like to have your world turned upside down.

"Yeah, we're missing our mama something fierce," Rusty whispered, his eyes beginning to shimmer with a telltale sheen that indicated just how deep and heartfelt this confusion was, too.

Wyatt nodded solemnly, chiming in sadly, "We haven't never been away from our mama this long. Our daddy, neither." His lower lip trembled slightly as he lay on his pillow and clutched his baseball mitt tightly to his chest.

Both boys looked so dejected and heartbroken, and Maggie didn't know quite what to say. The truth was, she had no idea when, or even if, both their parents would be back.

"But having you and our Unka Jake around is better," Rusty admitted after a moment as Maggie bent to tuck him in, too.

"Yeah, it's almost like being with our mama and daddy and having a real family," Wyatt agreed.

Rusty reached out and tucked his fingers in hers. "So tell us you won't be like the others," he pleaded in a soft lonesome voice that brought a lump to her throat. He pinned his gaze on hers hopefully as he, too, leaned forward and gave her a fierce and impromptu hug good-night. "Promise us you'll stay with us, Maggie," he urged emotionally. "Leastwise, 'til our mama gets back."

How could she refuse such sweetly uttered requests? Especially when she knew Jake and Harry couldn't begin to handle the boys alone. "I promise I won't leave you guys in the lurch," Maggie vowed, bending to kiss the top of each little boy's head in turn. Even if it meant putting up with the ornery Jake MacIntyre a few more weeks....

"THESE JUST ARRIVED for you, from your brother, via taxi," Jake said, meeting Maggie in the hall outside the boys' room.

Maggie grinned at the way Jake was loaded down with luggage.

"You didn't have to carry them all at once," she teased. He had a carry-on, flight bag and garment bag looped over his broad shoulders, plus a large Pullman suitcase in each hand. "Frankly, I don't know how you manage to stay upright with all that weight. I can hardly lug one of them around at a time."

"Understandable," he muttered, "considering they each weigh a ton. Didn't anyone ever tell you to travel light?"

"All the time. I never did." She reached for one of the bags, prepared to do her share. "Let me help you."

Jake shook his head and backed up, refusing to let her handle even the flight bag containing her makeup, hair dryer, hot rollers and toiletries. "I can manage." He inclined his head to the front of the ranch house. "This way. I'll show you your room."

Maggie glanced over her shoulder. "Shouldn't I sleep next to the boys?"

"I've got the bedroom on one side of them, my sister Kelsey and her husband, should they ever show up again," Jake told her gruffly, "have the room on the other side."

Maggie blinked, caught off guard by the inherent pessimism in his statement. "What do you mean, if?" she said, feeling both stunned and aghast as she stopped dead in her tracks. "I thought this was just a temporary arrangement, Jake."

Jake shrugged his broad shoulders aimlessly and continued swaggering down the hall. "As far as I know," he answered casually, "it is."

"But—" Without warning, Maggie's heart was pounding as she caught up with him.

Beneath the dark mustache, Jake's lips took on a cynical curve. "Let's just say I don't have my hopes pinned on a happy ending." He paused in front of an open doorway. "Be that as it may, I figured you might be happier down at this end of the house. It's quiet. You'll have your own bath and phone." He led the way into the rose-and-white bedroom, adding, "Harry's suite of rooms is just across the hall."

Good, Maggie thought. A chaperon!

Jake set her bags down with a thud. He looked her over and drawled, "You gonna meet Travis Benefield like that?"

Because all her clothes had gotten drenched in her impromptu dive into the swimming pool and she had initially brought nothing with her save the clothes on her back and her horse Buttercup, Maggie was now dressed entirely in Jake's clothes: a blue chambray work shirt, sleeves rolled up to the elbow, the long tails knotted at her waist, elastic-waisted dark green flannel boxer shorts from the Gap that came only to her upper thighs, and a pair of borrowed white sweat socks. She thought she looked just okay; considering the shirt was far too big across the shoulders, the boxers showed way too much leg and she had no shoes to wear at all. The look in his dark eyes said otherwise. She didn't think he could have appeared more admiring, had she been dressed to compete in the Miss America Pageant.

"'Cause I don't know how it'd go over, meeting him," Jake drawled, "if you're dressed in my clothes."

Nevertheless, Maggie had been thinking about it. Not because she wanted Travis Benefield to draw implications about her relationship with Jake. There was, after all, nothing to speculate about. No, she'd go as is just to let Mr. Travis Benefield know she didn't have to put on airs to meet any man, rich or not.

Aware Jake was staring, fascinated, at the length of suntanned leg exposed beneath the hem of his boxer shorts, Maggie tugged them a little lower down her thigh. "I suppose manners dictate I make some effort, since this is a first impression," Maggie murmured reluctantly.

Jake looked relieved she wasn't going to be wearing his boxer shorts, shirt and socks to meet Travis; she wondered if that was because he had figured out she hadn't anything on beneath them, since her undies had been drenched, too.

"I think I'd agree with you on that," he said.

Maggie opened one of her suitcases. She carried fistfuls of filmy lingerie to the bureau. Folding them neatly as was her custom, she put them in one item at a time. "What kind of a man is he?" she asked curiously, a little put out to be deviating from her already made, heavily researched wish list of hot prospects.

"Rich."

Jake suddenly seemed to be having trouble swallowing.

"Besides that," Maggie urged, wondering if it was the sight of the lingerie or the fact it was her lingerie, bothering him. Either option annoyed her, as she was tired of being regarded as just a pretty face and an incredible body. "What else do you know about Travis Benefield?" she asked impatiently.

Without warning Jake looked very irritated at her questions. "He's very busy. He's also always on time, so you better hurry. Meet you downstairs in five minutes?"

Maggie nodded, knowing it wasn't much time but she could manage. "I'll be there."

A BRIMMING GLASS of ice-cold Lone Star beer in hand, Jake was deep in conversation with Travis Benefield about the easiest ways to saddle break a horse when Maggie entered the room. "Jake, you didn't tell me you had company!" Travis said with a chuckle.

Jake swung around to see Maggie, and felt the air go out of his lungs.

He'd thought she was desirable as all get-out in borrowed shirt, boxers and socks. In a floaty white halter dress that stopped just above her knees, she was incredible. The soft fabric clung to her breasts and tiny waist with unerring accuracy. The backless design of the dress showed a wealth of creamy suntanned skin. High-heeled sandals made the most of her fabulously sexy legs. Just looking at her made his mouth grow dry and his lower body come alive in a way it hadn't been since... Hell, it had never felt quite that way. Which was another reason to get on with this, he thought sourly.

Mindful of his manners, he stepped forward to make introductions gracefully. "Travis Benefield, I'd like you to meet Maggie Porter. She's been helping me out with my nephews today. She's a New York fashion model."

"Don't I know that," Travis drawled, as he stood and stuck out an arthritic hand to shake Maggie's with heartfelt if overly enthusiastic gratitude. His leathery cheeks pinkening with masculine appreciation, Travis Benefield announced proudly to one and all, "I may not live in a bunkhouse any longer, but I didn't stop getting *Sports Illustrated* just 'cause I turned seventy."

"THAT WAS A LOUSY thing to do." Maggie turned on Jake the moment Travis Benefield left, two excruciatingly boring hours of small talk later. Although, she thought furiously, she should have known all along that the mischievous Jake would pull something like this on her.

Jake feigned innocence, much as she had expected he would, as he flattened a palm across his chest. "Hey," he defended himself, his dark eyes glittering with thinly veiled amusement. "You said you were looking for a husband. I have it on good authority that Travis is looking for a wife. Hence, I figured he'd be a really hot prospect for you."

Maggie sent him a withering glare.

Jake paused. In the spark-filled silence, he narrowed

his eyes at her speculatively, then asked with a naiveté she was sure was designed to grate on her nerves, "You're telling me you didn't like him?"

"Oh, for heaven's sake!" Maggie swore at Jake in exasperation. "I'm thirty years old, Jake. Travis Benefield might once have been a horse wrangler but he is also old enough to be my grandfather!"

"So..." Jake ruminated a moment as he smoothed the ends of his sable brown mustache. "Am I to deduce from this that men who are seventy and older are out, even if they are cowboys through and through and rich and eccentric to boot?"

Maggie clamped her arms in front of her defiantly. Only the knowledge that it would give him a great deal of satisfaction to see her completely lose her temper with him, kept her from decking him. "You bet your britches they are."

He grinned at the fire in her eyes. He leaned closer, and with a leering grin, said, "If age was a factor, Maggie honey, you should've said so to begin with."

Maggie followed his taunting words with another glacial look and the carefully worded admonition, "I'm mentioning it now. Do not introduce me to any men who are too old to be a father."

"Actually," Jake transferred his beer bottle to his other hand and stroked his ruggedly carved jaw to comic affect, "I'm pretty sure that Travis still has a few...uh...potential babies...in him, Maggie."

Like she didn't know that a gun could still fire even though it was old? Maggie exhaled, shut her eyes, and very slowly opened them again. "I'm not talking about the biological factors, Jake," she corrected sternly, refusing to so much as crack a smile. "I'm talking about the business of being a parent."

"Oh." Jake nodded as if a light had just suddenly gone on in a darkened room. "So what's the cutoff point then?" he asked helpfully, now that he was thusly illuminated.

"I don't know." Maggie regarded him with mounting exasperation as she began to pace. "How old are you?" He seemed about the right age.

"Thirty-two. But just so you know, Maggie honey, I'm not in the running for daddy anything," he said firmly.

One look in his dark brown eyes told her that was true. "Trust me," she said, quelling her inner disappointment, that was as much a surprise to her as it obviously was to him. "I have already deduced as much," she finished dryly. "And the answer is forty-five."

Jake blinked. "Forty-five what?"

"My cutoff age!" Maggie replied, irritated Jake couldn't seem to keep track of the conversation, when they were only talking about one thing. Advancing on him, she waved a lecturing finger beneath his nose. "So from this point on do not introduce me to anyone older than that," Maggie said firmly.

"Not even forty-five and a day?"

She refused to play his game.

Apparently aware her patience was at an end, Jake held up his hands in an age-old gesture of surrender. "Okay, okay. Don't get your knickers in a knot or go packing any suitcases just yet. We can work the kinks out of this arrangement."

"Can we?" Maggie regarded him, still unimpressed.

"Sure we can," he assured her smoothly, "if we discuss the...shall we say...*credentials*...you are looking for in a mate a little more thoroughly, before I go a'looking again."

"You mean my wish list?"

"Whatever you want to call it." Jake reached for a pen and paper.

While he sat at the writing desk, she circled closer. "First, any beau you set me up with has to be smart."

Jake made a disapproving face. "There's such a thing as being too smart, you know," he admonished.

"Not in my book." Maggie watched as Jake scribbled obediently. "And he has to be kind," she continued.

"A wimp then," Jake paraphrased as he scrawled "kind of wimpy?" on his copy of her alleged list.

"No, not a wimp." Maggie snatched the pen from his hand, crossed out *wimpy,* and wrote precisely what she'd wanted there in the first place. "Just kind." Maggie jotted down the word *kind.* "And nice." Maggie jotted down the word *nice.*

Jake squinted at her thoughtfully and screwed up his lips in comical fashion as she handed the pen to him.

"Sounds like you've just described a sissy."

"I have not!" Maggie countered, aware her blood pressure was beginning to rise once again.

"I disagree. If a guy is too nice, he tends to get run over in business and every other aspect of life. To be perfectly blunt, I don't really know any nice, kind millionaires, Maggie. None that are self-made, anyway."

Maggie could tell he was trying to stall her until she quit; nevertheless she remained undaunted. "I am sure there are some," she insisted, folding her arms in front of her, as the air conditioner clicked on and cool air poured out of vents overhead.

"Not who've made money the hard way," Jake disagreed, his eyes drifting to the way her folded arms pulled the chiffon fabric tightly across her breasts, defining the sensual curves and gathered nipples.

"Then look for someone who inherited," Maggie advised, exasperated, dropping her arms, but able to do nothing about the chill in the room or the effect the suddenly cool air had on her thinly clad breasts.

"Even less of a chance of an old money fella being nice," Jake said. His eyes fixed on her face, he continued, "'Cause all they're trying to do is hang on to their money. Why? 'Cause they don't know how to survive without it, and are afraid to try. So, nope, you're not going to have much luck there, either."

She glowered at him. "Are you trying to be helpful?" She stalked back and forth. "Because I swear, Jake 'honey,'" she said hotly, "it doesn't *sound* as if you are."

Jake let his glance drift down her legs, before slowly, slowly returning to her face. "If I was trying to be helpful, Maggie, *honey,* I would advise you to forget the marriage and just have a hot passionate affair. Less risk, less trouble, tons more pleasure."

Maggie glared at him, aware her heart had taken on a slow, heavy beat. "I am not an affair kind of woman, Jake," she warned.

But he wasn't buying it. "You might surprise yourself," Jake drawled.

The next thing Maggie knew he had closed the distance between them swiftly, and taken her in his arms. She didn't have to be a fortune-teller to know what was on his mind. Worse, the same thing was on hers and had been all evening. "Jake, damn it, you swore if I took care of the boys for you that you wouldn't hit on me," Maggie protested breathlessly, knowing even as she said it she didn't really want him to keep his hands to himself.

"I lied," he confessed, dancing her backward to the doors, which he shut and locked. Finished, he backed her to the wall. Hands braced on either side of her, he spread his legs on either side of hers, aligned his lower half with hers, and slowly pressed his chest to hers. "Besides, you're off duty now, when it comes to the boys, as they're asleep." He placed a light, tempting kiss to her brow. "Which means I'm off duty, too." Another kiss, this one to her cheek. "And since I temporarily no longer have to behave myself..." He kissed her again, on the neck, until Maggie quivered all over and groaned, soft and low in her throat.

He tunneled his hands through the silk of her hair and ever so deliberately tilted her face up to his. Eyes locked with hers, he vowed, "...I think I'll do what I've been wanting to do since the moment you walked downstairs wearing that piece of fabric you call a dress."

Determined to resist, Maggie drew a deep breath that lifted her breasts, and closed her eyes against his compelling gaze. "Jake, I—"

"That's it," he whispered back, as his mouth lowered slowly, inevitably to hers. "Say it, Maggie," he encouraged softly. "Say my name. Say it over and over again."

And then all was lost in the wonder of his kiss, in the feel of his tongue moving sensually across the seam of her lips. Maggie moaned again, shifting against him. His lower half was rigid with arousal. Where he pressed against her, the ache increased with lightning speed. Instantaneously, her insides went liquid and her knees weakened to a treacherous degree. "Oh, Jake," Maggie murmured again, as her fingers dug into his shoulders, and then his tongue was inside her mouth, sweeping sweetly, giving to her the kind of desire she had only dreamed existed. The yearning that swept through her was almost unbearable. Her breasts ached and burned for the nimble play of his fingers. Before she knew what she was doing, Maggie had threaded her hands through his hair and she was kissing him back, passionately, wildly, wantonly. Until everywhere their bodies touched, liquid fire pooled. Tormented beyond her wildest dreams, Maggie groaned again. His knee slid between hers even as his hand went to the catch that held up the front of her dress. Her lips parted. And she knew he was going to make love to her, here, now.

Make love...

But not marry...

Never marry...

Realizing how easily she could be seduced both by Jake and the chemistry flowing between them, realizing that if he loved her and then left her he really would break her heart, Maggie came swiftly to her senses. Her breath coming hard and fast, she tore her mouth from his, and with her hands flat across his chest, pushed him away from her. "Jake, stop!"

Too late, he had already undone her dress.

Working feverishly to save herself from what surely was a worse fate than her last broken engagement, Maggie caught the edges of her chiffon dress before the bodice could fall from her breasts. She could not help but be aware of the hard rasp of Jake's breath, the trembling of his body, nor the disappointment in his eyes, as she reclasped the catch at the nape of her neck with shaky fingers. Nor could she seem to take her eyes away from his.

"No seeing what's under that fabric, hmm?" Jake teased, his heated glance roving her breasts and making the sensitized tips pucker all the more. The yearning inside her increased, warring firmly with the urge to protect herself, until finally, inevitably, the age-old instinct for survival won out.

"Not a chance in hell," Maggie affirmed, uncomfortably aware even as she spoke that she'd like nothing more than to feel his lips on her breasts and that it would take very little—a few more hot, seasoned kisses—for him to seduce her into making love with him all night, all the way. In fact, to her detriment, she could even imagine how wonderful and wild it would be. And that, she knew, was not wise, either.

Looking extraordinarily pleased with himself, Jake stepped back and grinned down at her in a way that made her pulse race all the more. "So it won't happen tonight," he said breezily, with only a modicum of regret, looking suddenly smug and very male. His eyes darkened sensually as he leaned toward her and promised, "It will happen, Maggie. And it'll happen soon."

He seemed so damn sure of himself. And her! Maggie had half a mind to kiss him again, just to prove she could do so and still walk away. Yet even as she contemplated such a move, Maggie schooled herself to remember her end goal here and that was to be married and have a family of her own. Jake had already been quite forthright in telling her that he was not going to give that to her. Not now, not ever.

Which meant, like it or not, she had only one path to take.

"Like heck it will," she countered hotly to his assertion they would make love and soon. She smoothed her hair into place and drew her dignity around her like an invisible force that would keep him away. "From now on, cowboy, I am keeping you strictly at arm's length!"

Before Jake could reply, the phone rang. Jake swore heatedly, looking mighty unhappy at the interruption, and reached for the phone with a disgruntled frown. "Who could be calling this late at night?"

before they were dragged apart by security this
morning.'' The night bartender—who it seemed could
smell a con a mile away—

"Quiet!" the bouncer bellowed. "I did not ask for
comments from you!" He turned back to Jake, who—to
Maggie's dismay from her player vantage point in the
bedroom—was out for blood, and emotionally, when it
came to his kin and family, well able to stand his own
 and then some, too, no matter what his past reservations
about the Lockharts. "Now, mister," was the same
bouncer said ominously...

## Chapter Five

"Kelsey, thank God, where are you?" Jake demanded,
relieved his sister had at last called to check in.

"Colorado," Kelsey said.

Aware Maggie was starting to tiptoe out of the
room, Jake motioned for her to stay put. "What are
you doing there?" he asked his sister, his eyes still on
Maggie, who was looking deliciously tousled after
their kiss. Damn, but he wished he could kiss her again
and take her up to his bed and...

On the other end of the line, Kelsey let out an exasperated hiss. "I'm doing what I've been doing, looking for Clint!" she told him angrily.

Jake massaged the tension from the back of his
neck. Whether he liked it or not, Kelsey's situation
had to be dealt with. "Did you find Clint?" Jake
asked, realizing he was still a little angry, too.

"No, not yet," Kelsey admitted with a reluctant
sigh, "but I think I'm getting close."

That, Jake figured, was debatable. "I think you
should cut your losses and come home, Kelsey," he
ordered sternly, his fury with his proud-to-a-fault
brother-in-law intact. "The twins miss you."

Kelsey blew her nose. "Rusty and Wyatt miss their dad, too," she replied emotionally. "Furthermore, this is all your fault, Jake."

"Mine!" Jake echoed, incensed. "I'd like to know how you figure that!" All he had tried to do was help!

Kelsey ignored him, as she always did when he lost his temper with her. "I'll call tomorrow, when the boys are up," she said stiffly, as Jake closed his eyes and passed a hand over his eyes. "I just wanted you to know I'm okay," she continued in a low voice seething with resentment.

Jake sighed. He was handling this all wrong. God knew the last thing he wanted was to make things worse for her. "Kelsey—"

*Click.*

Realizing his younger sister had hung up on him, again, Jake swore beneath his breath. He opened his eyes, found Maggie looking at him with concern. Frowning, Jake hung up the phone.

"Problem?" Maggie asked, as he had known she would.

"And then some," Jake muttered regretfully, aware that as far as Kelsey and Clint went he could not do anything right.

"You know, I can go on upstairs and give you some space," Maggie offered.

Again, Jake shook his head. He wanted her to stay. "No. Don't. I could use a friend right now."

Maggie edged closer. "You and your sister were fighting just now?"

Jake nodded sadly. He took her hand and led her over to the sofa. "It's become a real habit, as of late."

Maggie kicked off her sandals and curled up next

to him on the sofa. Her blue eyes sympathetic, she regarded him kindly. "Because you don't approve of the man she married, I gather?"

"How do you—?"

"It was obvious, in the disparaging way you spoke of her husband, Clint, and urged her to cut her losses and come home. Honestly, Jake, you can't expect her to appreciate that."

"Yeah, well." Jake turned toward Maggie slightly, so his thigh nudged her knee. "I don't appreciate being blamed for the breakup of her marriage."

Maggie absently smoothed a speck of lint from the shoulder seam on his shirt, then dropped her hand back to the sofa as she looked into his eyes and asked in a soft, nonjudgmental tone, "Were you responsible?"

Jake shook his head. "No. Although I would have prevented the marriage in the first place, if I could have. It was the year my dad died. I was twenty, Kelsey was eighteen. I knew she was upset but I never expected her to decide not to go to college and run off with her boyfriend, Clint, and elope. By the time I found out about it, the damage was done. She was married and determined to stay married and she followed Clint from one ranching job to the next, making the best home she could for them, and eventually the twins."

"What's not to like so far?" Maggie interrupted. "They both sound pretty responsible and family-oriented to me."

"They were until about a year ago when the ranch Clint was managing was sold and he suddenly lost his job."

"He couldn't find another?" Maggie guessed.

Jake took Maggie's hand in his and absently stroked the inside of her wrist. "Nothing comparable to what Clint'd had, as a ranch manager for a big spread. Kelsey offered to go to work to support the family until he could find something like what he'd had but Clint wouldn't hear of it. He felt she should be home with the boys. So I stepped in and offered him a job on the Rollicking M. He told me he didn't want my charity and refused it. He wanted to wait until he found a good job on his own, with comparable salary and a few benefits. Only problem was, by then their savings had run out and they were ready to lose their house. I offered to loan them the money to keep it—again, it was refused. So I did the only thing I could; I offered to call in every influential friend I knew in the Cattlemen's Association and get him a job that way. Again, I was refused. So I did it on the sly."

To his chagrin, Maggie looked every bit as aghast as his sister and her husband had been about that. "Oh, no, Jake, you didn't," she said.

Beginning to feel really angry all over again, Jake dropped her hand and clenched his jaw. "What was I supposed to do, let my sister and her two boys starve because her husband is too proud and stubborn to accept my help?"

Maggie couldn't argue that. "So what happened?"

"Clint took the job that I'd gotten for him. He was doing great, too. It was working out for everyone until a jealous co-worker who knew someone who knew someone else told Clint he'd been hired as a favor to me. Clint was furious. He verified that was indeed the case, quit, and went home and told Kelsey what I'd done."

"Did she know?"

Jake shook his head. "No. Up until that point, she hadn't a clue. I didn't tell her because I didn't want to put her in a position of keeping something like that from Clint."

Silence fell as Maggie took all that in. "How did she feel?"

"She was royally ticked off."

"So they ran away together and left the boys with you?" Maggie guessed.

"No." Again, Jake shook his head. "Clint took off to find his own job without my influence or interference. He told Kelsey he was heading north to the big spreads in Colorado, Montana, and the Dakotas to look for a position as good as the one he'd had. He told her she wouldn't hear from him again until that had happened. Kelsey figured he'd either find something quickly or cool off and come back to her and the boys and continue looking here in Texas, but when he hadn't returned after two months, she decided to go looking for him herself. So, she borrowed some money from a friend, left the twins with me and went off to find him. That was a couple weeks ago. Since she still hasn't found him, I asked her to come home. That's what we were arguing about just now. Not surprisingly, she refused. She's just as stubborn and foolishly independent as Clint is."

Maggie's blue eyes were filled with understanding.

"Sounds like you have a real mess on your hands."

"Yep. Kelsey blames me for interfering with her marriage, and she says she isn't coming home until she has righted my wrong and brought her husband back."

Maggie was silent a long moment. "She must really love her husband, to forgive him running out on her like that."

"I've never doubted that..." Jake admitted. In fact, it was one of the things he envied about his sister and her husband, the fact they did love each other so.

"But...?" Maggie studied his face.

He shrugged, unable to help but be angry about all the time Clint and Kelsey were wasting. Crises should be handled together, as a family unit, not apart.

"I know what it's like to love someone so much you'd lay your life down for them, but I still don't think that gives either Clint or Kelsey just cause to run out on the boys the way they have, even temporarily."

Maggie laid her hand on his. "Still, it's probably better that she and her husband work out their difficulties in private, don't you think?"

"I guess," Jake studied their intertwined fingers. Her hand looked so soft and delicate next to his. Sighing, Jake turned his gaze to Maggie's face and admitted, "I wouldn't want the boys to witness the arguments between Clint and Kelsey if she can't talk some sense into him and bring him back. And I've got some doubts about whether or not Kelsey will be successful in her endeavor."

"How come?" Maggie asked, her blond eyebrows furrowing in concern.

Jake sighed and wished it wasn't true. "Because Clint's a cowboy through and through."

"Meaning?" Maggie prodded.

Jake shrugged. "Clint's never been happy on any one ranch for long. He's always looking for greener pastures, more of a challenge."

"Sounds a bit like you."

Jake warned himself not to get too attached to the admiration in her eyes. "I'll admit my life has been defined by hard work, too. And that I'm also a solitary kind of guy who takes a lot of satisfaction from saddling up and roaming the range. But I draw the line at putting my profession before my family."

"And you think that's what Clint is doing?" Maggie asked gently.

"It's what most cowboys do," Jake replied emphatically. "That's why so many never marry at all, 'cause they can't settle down for long, even when they try."

"You say that almost as if you accept it," Maggie noted, clearly troubled by the revelation.

"That's because I do accept it," Jake replied. The moment drew out. He gave her a steady, assessing look. "So, do you still want to lasso yourself a cowboy?" he asked lightly. "Or are you aiming for someone a little easier to tie down?"

"Like what?" Maggie asked, a flirtatious light suddenly reflected in her deep blue eyes. "A desk jockey or a stockbroker?"

"Anyone who doesn't spend their life roaming the wide-open range," Jake specified bluntly.

"Actually, I think now that I've considered it a bit, what I really want is a Renaissance cowboy."

That sounded like something that someone who'd lived in New York too long would come up with, Jake thought, smothering a laugh. "And what would that be?" he asked.

"In my particular case, a Texan who is good at, and interested in, just about everything."

"Hmm." Jake regarded her thoughtfully as she continued to look at him.

"Although when it comes to your sister and her problems, you're more understanding than I thought," she allowed. "For a Neanderthal cowboy, that is."

He narrowed his gaze at her. The mischief sparkling in her long-lashed eyes brought out an answering devilry in him. "That what you think of me?" Jake prodded back. "That I'm a Neanderthal?" Somehow the knowledge wasn't as disturbing to him as he thought it should be. Maybe because she seemed to bring out the caveman instincts inside him.

"It was," Maggie admitted. "Until you said you knew what it was like to love someone so much you'd lay your life down for them, anyway." Maggie pinned him with her eyes. "So who was she, Jake?" she demanded with unassailable determination and curiosity. "Who was the woman you would've laid your life down for?"

MAGGIE WAITED for Jake's answer. To her frustration, he merely grinned evasively and taunted teasingly, "Jealous, darlin'?"

"Curious," Maggie corrected, still holding his eyes deliberately when he would've put her off.

Jake disengaged their entwined hands and stood. "Curiosity killed the cat," he announced as he stalked away from her.

"But not me," Maggie replied as she uncurled her legs from beneath her and stood.

In fact, thus far, her need to discover things for herself had always been an asset. And she wanted to know who Jake had been in love with. Might still be in love with...

"I beg to differ with you on that, Maggie honey. In this case, your curiosity just might be your downfall." He watched as she bent and picked up her sandals. "Don't you think you ought to be hitting the sack?" he suggested in a not-so-subtle ploy to be rid of her and her nosy questions. "Those nephews of mine are likely to be up pretty early."

Maggie pursed her lips in silent frustration. It didn't take a rocket scientist to figure out Jake wasn't going to tell her what she wanted to know tonight. Hence, she would just have to find out what kind of romantic past he'd had from other sources. Perhaps, Harry.

Smiling resolutely, she bid him good-night. "I'll see you tomorrow, cowboy." She sauntered toward the door, then hand on the knob, turned to face him. "About those other beaus you owe me. I trust none of the others will be over seventy?" she asked, letting him know with a determined glance they had better not be!

Looking relieved to be talking about something other than himself again, Jake flashed her his bad-boy grin and promised, "You can count on it."

"ABOUT TIME WE connected," Maggie told her friend Clarissa on the telephone, half an hour later. Too wired after the kisses and conversation to sleep, she'd elected to talk on the phone instead, and had called her brother Billy to check in, only to find a message waiting for her there, too, from Clarissa, and at long last, a way to get in touch with her again. "I haven't heard from you for so long I was beginning to get worried sick about you, Clarissa!" Maggie continued.

"I'm sorry it's taken me so long," Clarissa apologized readily. "I wanted to get settled in Chicago before I telephoned you. Then I found out from your brother that you were in the process of settling somewhere else too—in Texas, this time."

"I'm trying to decide where in Texas I want to live," Maggie said.

"Where are you now?" Clarissa asked.

"I'm taking care of a rancher's little nephews—"

"Baby-sitting?"

Briefly, Maggie filled in Clarissa on how and why she'd come to meet up with Jake MacIntyre.

"Well, Maggie, you always have liked to live life on the edge," her flame-haired friend teased, when Maggie had finished her recitation.

Maggie laughed, then paused. Usually when Clarissa moved, it meant there'd been some kind of trouble. And right now, Maggie's radar for problems was sounding a red alert. "Are you doing okay?" Maggie asked Clarissa gently. It wasn't like Clarissa to completely lose touch with them and never for this long. Usually, no matter what was going on in their lives, they talked every couple of weeks on the phone.

"Yes and no. There's no easy way to say this. Maggie, I finally did it. I—I got a divorce."

"Oh, Clarissa." Maggie sighed, her heart going out to her old friend. This had to be a rough time. And it was just like Clarissa to be embarrassed her relationship with her ex hadn't worked out and think she had to shoulder the whole burden alone.

"You're probably thinking I should have done it long ago," Clarissa asserted.

Maggie knew she wouldn't do either of them any favors by being less than honest. "Your ex-husband never did treat you and Tommy right."

"Well, things are looking up now," Clarissa announced cheerfully, "because I've got a teaching job, a baby-sitter Tommy loves—his name is Conor James—and I've finally found that millionaire Sabrina predicted I would marry. His name is Fred Tannenbaum, and he's asked me to marry him."

Maggie wanted Clarissa to be happy. Heaven knew she deserved to be. "That's great, Clarissa! I look forward to meeting him. Furthermore, it's funny you should mention Sabrina," Maggie said, twisting the phone cord around her index finger. "Because I saw her in New York, right before I left."

"You're kidding!" Clarissa enthused. "I saw her, too, on the last day of the SummerFest carnival in Bridgeport."

Maggie ran a hand through her hair. "Next thing we know, Hallie will claim to have seen Sabrina, too," Maggie joked.

"What if she did?" Clarissa whispered.

What indeed? Maggie wondered. "There's only one thing to do," Maggie said. "I'm calling Hallie!"

Determined to find out, she telephoned her cousin Hallie in Chicago as soon as she got off the phone, and got her machine.

"Hi, this is Hallie. Leave a message and I'll call you back when I can."

The machine beeped, letting Maggie know it was okay to begin her message.

"Hallie, it's Maggie in Texas. Call me at Jake MacIntyre's ranch in Texas." Maggie relayed the number and hung up.

"SO WHAT'RE WE GONNA DO today that's specially entertaining?" Rusty demanded at breakfast the next morning.

"I'd like to hear the answer to that myself," Jake drawled as he passed the platter of scrambled eggs.

Maggie glanced out the kitchen windows. It was a beautiful day. The sun was shining brightly. Fluffy white clouds dotted the pale blue sky. A warm breeze was shaking the leafy green trees. She knew, in an instant, she wanted to be outdoors. And so probably did the twins. "Do you guys like kites?" she asked.

Rusty and Wyatt shrugged in unison.

"Don't know. Never tried it," Rusty piped.

"Well, how about we go into town today—if Jake'll let me borrow one of the ranch vehicles—"

"You can take my Jeep," he said.

"Thanks." Maggie smiled at him, aware that between the kids and the ranch, she sort of felt as though she were on vacation, too. "And we'll buy a couple of kites, assemble them and see if we can get them to fly. All before lunch," Maggie decreed.

"Cool," Wyatt said, grinning from ear to ear.

"Way cool," Rusty agreed.

"Do you guys need help?" Maggie asked, noting they were still clad in their Texas Rangers pajamas.

"Nope. We'll be fine," Wyatt told her, while Rusty nodded that this was indeed so.

"Okay. Don't forget to brush your teeth and comb

your hair before you come down," Maggie said. "As soon as you boys're ready, we'll go."

They took off. Jake stood, dressed in jeans, boots and a work shirt, looking reluctant to leave. "How much do you know about kites?" he asked Maggie.

*More than I know about your past love life,* Maggie thought, aware she was still quite frustrated on that score. "Plenty. I used to amuse my three brothers, Deke, Billy and Frank with them in Central Park, when we all lived in New York."

Jake grinned. "I'd like to meet them someday."

Maggie smiled. "That can probably be arranged."

He reached into his pocket and brought out a handful of bills. He tossed them down in front of Maggie. "For the kites and whatever else you think the boys need or would enjoy."

Maggie pocketed the money in her jeans. "I'll bring you a receipt."

"You don't have to do that."

Didn't she? Given the way she had researched him and sought him out, he already thought she was a gold digger. "I insist," she said quietly. Before she left here he would know, no matter how things appeared, that she was not after his money and never had been.

Their eyes met, held. Without warning, Maggie was reminded of their passionate kisses. She could tell by the look in his eyes that Jake recalled them, too.

Frowning, Jake grabbed his hat and tugged it low on his brow. "Harry, I'm going out to check on the cattle. We've got a couple of sick steers, in need of attention. Call me on the cell phone, if you need me."

Without another word or even a glance in her direction, Jake swaggered purposefully out the door, letting it bang behind him.

Harry Wholesome and Maggie were left alone in the kitchen. Maggie stood and began to clear the breakfast dishes.

Harry, who was dressed in a casual sport shirt and slacks, looked sheepishly at Maggie. She could tell that he at least had come to respect her, probably due to the way she cared for the boys. "About my, er...ah, masquerade yesterday—" Harry began awkwardly.

"You and Jake pull that shenanigan often?" Maggie teased, letting Harry know with a smile she considered there was no harm done.

Harry admitted reluctantly, "When it comes to women, more often than I care to say. You'd be surprised how many actually act interested in me, in lieu of Jake, until they find out who I really am."

"Oh, I have a feeling you have your share of lady friends," Maggie drawled. To women his age, a man like Harry would probably be quite a catch.

Harry merely grinned at Maggie, acknowledging this was so. And that he, like Jake, generally reveled in his attention from the opposite sex.

"What about Jake? Does he date?" Maggie asked.

Harry shrugged and began to wash dishes in earnest. "He squires women around here and there," he replied evasively.

Maggie slanted Harry a glance while she wiped the table clean with a sudsy rag. "But there's been no one serious since he had his heart broken?" she asked, curious.

Harry was so startled he nearly dropped a dish. He

whirled on Maggie, demanding, "What do you know about that?"

"Obviously, not enough," Maggie responded, sure she was on to something now. "That's it, isn't it?" she crowed victoriously. "That's why Jake doesn't date! He fell madly in love with some woman. She broke his heart. And he's never gotten over it."

"Anything you learn on that score, you're going to have to learn from Jake," Harry warned, putting up a palm to ward off further questions.

"But I'm right, aren't I?" Maggie pressed resolutely.

To her frustration, Harry merely set his jaw and didn't reply. Silence fell between them. Once again, Maggie knew what it was like to hit a stone wall.

"Hey, Maggie! We're ready to go get kites!" the boys said, as they raced back in the kitchen.

Wordlessly, Harry reached into a drawer and tossed her a set of keys. Without warning, he looked relieved to be getting rid of Maggie and all her questions, too, at least temporarily. "It's the dark green Jeep Wagoneer in the garage," Harry told her, turning away. "Lunch is at noon. Don't be late."

"HOW'RE THE STEERS?" Harry asked a dusty, dirty Jake as he stomped in the back door and peeled off his sweat-soaked shirt at the kitchen sink.

"Sufferin'." Jake wiped his brow with a swipe of his forearm. "The medicine we got from the vet should help, though."

Harry handed Jake a tall glass of lemonade. "You missed lunch."

Jake scowled, knowing as well as Harry that had

been no accident. "Yeah, well, there was more to do out there than I thought there'd be," he muttered.

Harry, acting more surrogate father than house-keeper now, gave him a questioning look. "Sure it's not her you're avoiding?" Harry jerked his head in the direction of the backyard, where Maggie and the boys were running back and forth, laughing and shouting and pulling two long-tailed kites on strings.

"She really does know what she's doing," Jake murmured, trying his best not to notice how long and lissome and downright sexy her legs were beneath the denim shorts.

"In more than one area, it would seem," Harry said dryly.

And then, sure his employer should know, Harry proceeded to tell Jake about his conversation with Maggie in the kitchen that morning.

"HEY, GUYS," Jake told his nephews half an hour and one long hot shower later. "Harry has some ices for you in the kitchen."

"All right!" Rusty and Wyatt dropped their kites and ran off to get them.

Maggie barely had time to catch the kite strings. With a curious look at Jake, she wordlessly handed him one kite, and began to reel in the one she kept in her hands.

He struggled to keep his matter-of-fact mood. It wasn't easy with her golden hair flowing like silk over her shoulders and the sun pinkening her cheeks. Not to mention the way she looked in the prim white sneakers, clinging T-shirt and the brief denim shorts.

"You want to talk to me?" Maggie edged close enough he could smell the scent of her perfume.

Jake frowned and concentrated on reeling in his kite. "I don't have any true confessions to make," he said sarcastically, "if that's what you mean."

Maggie's chin set determinedly but she did not look surprised. "Harry told you I asked him questions, didn't he?"

Jake nodded. "He was protecting me, and yes, he did."

Maggie tossed her head. Silky blond hair flew in every direction. "Well, you needn't worry 'cause he didn't tell me anything about your past love life, either," Maggie stormed.

"That's good." In fact, Jake was glad she was frustrated.

Maggie lifted a skeptical brow. "I'm not so sure it is," she said silkily, as she brought her kite in to within twenty feet of her. "Obviously, you haven't gotten over whatever happened in the past, if just the hint of it makes you this touchy."

"And obviously, if you are this nosy, and this interested in something that is none of your business, then you need distracting," Jake told her emphatically as he too continued to reel in his kite.

"And how would you plan to accomplish that, Jake?" Maggie taunted, a wealth of temper shimmering in her vivid blue eyes. "By kissing me again?"

Jake moved back, as swiftly and surely as if he had been burned. As tempting as her dare was, there was no way in hell he was doing that. She was getting under his skin much too swiftly as it was. Much more and...well, he didn't want to think about that. "You have a date coming for dinner," he announced, bringing his kite in so suddenly, it fell to the ground.

"Tonight?" Maggie reeled hers in gently, until she was able to catch it and lower it carefully to the ground.

Jake nodded.

"Mac Malone will be here at six sharp," he told her determinedly, knowing that if this didn't push Maggie Porter away from him and out of his life, nothing would.

"So have yourself and the boys ready. They'll need to wear their jackets and ties." Jake smiled, smugly predicting, "It's going to be quite an evening."

# Chapter Six

Quite an evening was right, Maggie thought, as she surveyed the boys, who were busy being just about as uncooperative as little boys could be.

"I hate ties."

"See?" Rusty pulled his to the side and made awfully authentic gagging noises. "Mine is already choking me!"

"And this jacket is even worse." Wyatt did a rude approximation of a chicken flapping its wings to demonstrate how uncomfortable he was. "It feels stiff and scratchy."

"Why do we have to go, anyway?" Rusty complained unhappily, plopping on Maggie's bed.

"Because your uncle Jake said," she replied firmly as she finished spritzing on her perfume. Jake had made it pretty clear by the way he'd come on to her that he thought she'd been dressed too sexy the evening before. Well, she'd be damned if Jake could find anything wrong with the way she dressed tonight. Her long stretch velvet dress with its fitted turtleneck bodice, long slim sleeves, lower calf-length skirt and demure princess seams, had her primly covered from her chin nearly to her ankles.

"Yeah, but, couldn't we just eat dinner in our rooms or something?" Wyatt protested.

Good point, Maggie thought as she sat to slip on her suede evening sandals and knot the thin bowties across her ankle. Why Jake was making two rambunctious little boys sit through a formal dinner was beyond her. But, seeing as she was merely the babysitter-for-barter it really wasn't her place to object. She put down her perfume and turned to her two charges.

"You're going because your Uncle Jake wants you there," she explained as they ambled over to stand on either side of her.

Pausing briefly, she straightened Rusty's tie and adjusted Wyatt's shirt collar, so it lay flat. "So how about this?" When all else failed, Maggie thought, resort to bribery again. After all, what difference did it make why the two boys behaved as long as they got in the habit of doing so? "If the two of you concentrate on behaving tonight, just like your uncle Jake has asked you to—"

"Just like Jake said," Wyatt interrupted helpfully, his brows furrowing together, as he urged Maggie to be even more specific about what was expected of them in the bound-to-be-boring evening ahead.

"Yes." Maggie nodded firmly, knowing that Jake had already had a talk with the boys while he supervised their showers earlier. "Then you two boys and I will do something very special tomorrow, too. Something even better than kites." Though what that was, Maggie didn't know.

"I don't know," Rusty paused, flattening a hand on

his just-combed hair and inadvertently messing up the neatly sectioned part. Briefly, he looked troubled. Or maybe it was just confused. "Unka Jake...well, I mean he told us what to do—" Rusty stammered uncertainly.

"Yeah, he sure did," Wyatt chimed in, nodding.

"Then just do it," Maggie said, maintaining a most positive attitude in the hopes the boys would follow her example and do the same. She took them both by the hand and encouraged softly, "Just do exactly what your uncle Jake said and everything will be fine, I promise you."

Rusty and Wyatt exchanged glances that were half baffled, half anxious. Finally, they both shrugged their small shoulders. It was clear, Maggie thought, they had very little experience in dress-up dinners. "Okay, Maggie," they agreed finally, nodding their heads. "We'll do exactly what you and our unka Jake say."

DAMN IT ALL, she didn't have to look so gorgeous all the time, did she? Jake thought irritably as Maggie descended the wide front staircase at six sharp, Wyatt on one side of her, Rusty on the other.

The boys were cute of course, in their identical navy blazers and striped ties, khaki pants and white shirts. But it was Maggie who took his breath away. Her espresso-colored velvet dress hugged her curvaceous form like a made-to-order glove. Her ridiculously flimsy shoes only added to her air of sexy yet untouchable allure. She had brushed her honey blond hair away from her face. It illuminated the sun-kissed hue of her fair skin and fell in a shimmering golden veil over her shoulders and partway down her back. Jake didn't know if it was the time she'd spent outdoors playing with the boys or simply the flattering dark color of her dress contrasted with the fairness of her skin, but her eyes had never seemed a more vivid blue than they did at that moment, her lips more voluptuous and naturally pink.

Judging from the asthmatic intake of their guest's breath, she took her date's breath away, too.

"Maggie," Jake said and forced himself to smile as he put his irritation aside and began the required introductions. "I'd like you to meet Mac Malone. His family owns a ranch in the next county."

"How do you do." Smiling cordially, Maggie shook Mac's hand.

If she was put off by Malone's slightly sleazy appearance, she did not show it, Jake noted, not sure how he felt about that, either.

When Mac didn't immediately let go of Maggie's hand, but instead held on to her palm unnecessarily, it was all Jake could do not to deck him for conduct unbecoming.

Telling himself he had to calm down if this evening was going to serve the purpose he intended, and prove a point about love, Jake stepped in, cutting smoothly and deliberately between Maggie and Mac.

Forcing Mac to let go of Maggie's hand, Jake took Maggie's elbow gallantly, and smiled at Mac and the boys. "Let's all go into the dining room. Shall we?"

MAGGIE KNEW the moment she saw Mac Malone that he was not the man for her. It wasn't just the black suede Western-tailored suit, complete with starched white shirt, and string tie, the Vegas rodeo clasp on his big-buckled belt, or his handcrafted alligator boots; it was the slightly snobbish, movie cowboy air about him.

He was, quite frankly, a fake.

He was also a guest in Jake's home.

Manners dictated she be as nice as could be.

She just wished she could say the same about Jake. He had been acting jealous as heck the whole evening—which was ridiculous when you thought about it, since he had no plans to marry her himself, or any woman for that matter. But there he was, acting as fiercely protective as an overbearing father overseeing his daughter's first date. Not that this was their only problem. Mac Malone had turned out to be the most boring, self-involved conversationalist she'd ever come across. Worse, she had never seen the twins more out of control, Maggie thought, frowning as Wyatt shot a pea at Rusty when Jake's head was turned.

Maggie reached out, caught the pea in midair before it tapped Rusty on the nose. Rusty giggled. She frowned at the twins and gave them a stern look that said, "Behave!" Meanwhile, Mac was completely oblivious as he rambled on to Jake, "And I just told the executor, that even if it was what my dad wanted, I can't live on a ranch. No way. Not in this day and age. Dallas is the place for me...."

"Of course, you, Maggie, have been all over the world," Mac continued, impressed.

"True," Maggie said.

Jake unceremoniously cut in. "And, according to the press, dated everyone who was anyone, too."

"Don't believe everything you read about me,"

Maggie said, speaking more to Jake now than Mac. "Not even half of it."

"But I've seen the photos," Mac said, capturing Maggie's attention yet again. "Of you and countless guys."

"Most of whom were friends. Or in some cases, complete strangers who just happened to get caught in the shot with me," Maggie explained, working to quell her aggravation for the sake of politeness. She had returned to Texas to avoid conversations such as this.

"Still, if you give up modeling you'll probably miss the attention, won't you?" Mac said, beginning to look just a tad concerned about Maggie's much-stated wish to lead a more low-profile, ordinary life.

Had Mac secretly been hoping to cash in on her celebrity, too? Maggie wondered uncomfortably, knowing there was no way in hell she was going through *that* again. "I won't miss the attention at all," Maggie answered Mac emphatically. She followed up her words with a determined look. "In fact, the only time I want my name to be in the newspaper from now on is if the news pertains to either my wedding or the birth of the children I intend to have."

"Hmm," Mac said, again looking less than pleased.

Another pea shot by. This time, Jake saw. But pretended not to.

Maggie drew a breath. She didn't know what had gotten into the boys, only that the soup and salad courses had been hellish. But the main course was turning out to be really excruciating, in all respects!

"Hey, he hit me!" Rusty claimed loudly, peeling the slightly squished pea off the lapel of his blazer.

Jake, who looked quite dashing himself, in a navy blazer, striped blue-and-white shirt, and tie, didn't reprimand them as Maggie expected. Instead, he put both his elbows on the table and grinned affectionately at his two trouble-making nephews. "Aren't they cute," he waxed affectionately to one and all. Turning back to a disapproving Mac Malone, Jake continued, "Maggie wants lots of kids, you know, and right away. But that's probably okay with you, isn't it, Mac, 'cause it's nothing new."

Maggie froze. Nothing new? "What are you talking about?" she asked Jake, intuiting only that he was quite obviously up to something Miss Manners would not sanction. And she'd thought the boys were misbehaving!

"Mac already has a lot of kids, don't you, Mac?"

Mac smiled uncomfortably. He tugged at the knot of his black string necktie. "No need to get into that now," he said.

"Trust me," Jake reassured with a merrily provoking smile. "Maggie'd want to know you have seven kids by six wives at only thirty-four."

"I've been married only five times, and I'm thirty-two," Mac corrected, looking slightly irritated—an emotion he tried to hide.

"Sorry. I get confused." Jake waved it off as Harry brought in a tray of sumptuous-looking desserts and set them on the sideboard. The boys, seeing treats were at hand, immediately straightened up.

Maggie turned back to Mac, not sure if he and Jake were pulling her leg. Mac was a jerk, no doubt about it, but he was also almost too self-aggrandizing to be real. "You have seven children?" she asked, eyes widening.

Mac nodded. "But I wouldn't mind a few more. They're really not much trouble."

A plant that required watering every other day wasn't "much trouble," Maggie thought. She gazed at Mac, able to see to her horror, that he was serious about the impact—or more correctly, lack of impact— his children had made on his life. "What an odd way to put it," Maggie told Mac politely, accepting the homemade peach cobbler and ice cream Harry set in front of her with a quiet thanks.

"Sounds good, huh, Maggie?" Jake said with a provoking grin. "The guy's young. Shooting—" Jake shot a glance at his nephews, who were so busy digging into their dessert they were oblivious to the conversation "—well, let's just say not blanks."

Maggie's jaw dropped in outrage. To her horror, Mac Malone merely chuckled. Mac looked at Maggie speculatively. "I don't know about another marriage. The alimony thus far is killing me. But as for the rest, if you're in that much of a hurry to have kids of your own, well…Jake's right, I have had a lot of success in that regard."

Maggie kicked Jake, who was beginning to chuckle, under the table. "I'm not in a hurry at all," she fibbed. At least not in that much of a hurry.

Maggie could have sworn Harry muttered the words *Good thing* while he coughed lightly behind her. Harry exited the dining room.

"This looks delicious, but I don't know." Mac patted his slightly paunchy middle. "I've got to watch my girlish figure," he joked.

At that, it was all Maggie could do not to roll her eyes.

"Hey, did you hear that?" Rusty shouted abruptly, having finished his dessert. "Mr. Malone said he's got a figure like a girl!" He and Wyatt hooted with laughter. The twins looked at Jake—who to Maggie's amazement was looking almost pleased by his nephews' rowdiness—and they hooted even louder. Mac reddened. His pompous jaw set.

"Boys—" Maggie began, knowing it was unpardonable to insult a guest you had invited into your home, and Jake had invited him, damn him. Meanwhile, Jake was strangely quiet as a peach slice flew by and landed on Rusty's cheek with such a gross splat that Maggie gasped in dismay. Looking quite unamused by the hit, Rusty pushed back his chair. Before she knew it, both boys were under the table, and brawling madly.

Jake just sat in his chair and shook his head with a boys-will-be-boys look.

"Jake, for heaven's sake, do something!" Maggie said.

"Oh, right." Jake snapped his fingers. "You want to be alone with Mac. Okay. Boys!" Jake whistled shrilly enough to stop traffic on 42nd Street. Their heads popped out from beneath the dining room table. "What, Unka Jake?"

"I think it's time to go upstairs, get in your pj's and watch TV in your room, don't you?"

They shrugged. "'Kay."

Wyatt and Rusty scrambled out from under the table, and dusted themselves off as best they could. Considering their ties were askew, their shirttails out, their hair a rumpled mess, the brushing off didn't do much.

"Nice to meet you, Mr. Malone," they said in unison.

"Yeah, we're sorry if we insulted you. We just...we got carried away or somethin'. Right, Uncle Jake?" Rusty looked at Jake for confirmation.

Jake nodded, looking awfully pleased with the boys, considering the scene they had just made. A scene that never would have been permitted under normal circumstances.

Maggie studied them silently, knowing something was definitely up, even if Mac Malone didn't.

His expression all innocence, Jake put a hand on the boys' shoulders and said, "I'll see you two in a bit."

Together, the trio leisurely exited the dining room.

"ALONE AT LAST," Mac Malone told Maggie as he pushed to his feet energetically. He lifted his brows in a suggestive manner that made her want to belt him one. "Perhaps we could go somewhere a little cozier?" Mac suggested, leering.

And give him the opportunity to put his hands on her? Maggie thought not. "Actually, Mac, I have a headache coming on. I'm sorry." She pressed a hand to her temple. Much more of Mac Malone's company and she would not have to fake a migraine. "I'm going to have to insist we cut the evening short."

Mac looked quite disappointed. "Some other time then?" he asked. "Perhaps tomorrow? We could drive into Dallas, have lunch."

"I don't think so. But thank you." Maggie caught sight of Harry Wholesome in the hall. She had never been so glad to see him. "Harry, would you be a dear and show Mr. Malone out?" she asked. She pressed her hand against her temple, aware her head was indeed beginning to throb at just the thought of spending one more minute with Mac Malone. "I have to take some aspirin."

Leaving Harry to deal with Mac, Maggie exited through the dining room to the kitchen.

BY THE TIME Maggie had located the aspirin, and taken two, Harry was in the kitchen.

"You will be relieved to know that Mr. Malone has left," he told her kindly.

Maggie gulped another half glass of water and sighed. "Thanks, Harry. I'm sorry I acted like the lady of the manor just now. I only asked you to show him out—"

"So he wouldn't try to kiss you good-night. I know. A perfectly understandable sentiment, in my opinion, if you don't mind my saying so."

"I don't." Maggie paused, then pitched in to help Harry with the dishes. "Is Mac a *friend* of Jake's?" Somehow, she just couldn't picture it.

"No. Not at all," Harry said, loading the dishwasher with amazing speed. "In fact the two of them have never really liked each other, as far as I could tell. They were just thrown together in an investment group or two, years ago, when Jake was just getting started building up his own portfolio."

"Then why did he invite him to have dinner with all of us tonight?" Maggie asked. "Instead of just fixing me up on a blind date with Mac that would take place elsewhere?'' Why had Jake made the boys dress up and sit through the excruciatingly boring dinner?

"I think Jake was trying to be helpful, by personally overseeing your first meeting with Mr. Malone," Harry explained carefully, after a moment.

Maggie knew a snow job when she heard one. Helpful, hah! "Trying to be helpful or teach me a lesson?" Maggie asked, as she washed out the coffeepot and put the cream and sugar away.

In response to her question, Harry only smiled. But then he didn't need to say anything, as Maggie already knew the answer.

FEELING IMMEASURABLY better, now that Mac Malone was gone and her aspirin had started to work, Maggie headed up the stairs. Jake was in the room with his nephews. They had already changed into their pajamas and were happily sprawled beneath their covers, watching a baseball game on TV.

Their uncle Jake was lounging in an overstuffed arm chair in the corner, his feet propped up on a toy chest he had dragged over to act as ottoman. Though still in his dinner clothes, he had removed his jacket, loosened the knot of his tie and unbuttoned the first two buttons on his shirt. He looked sexy and approachable in an unutterably masculine way. His sable eyes sparkled as she paused in the doorway. "Finished already?" Jake drawled, clasping his hands together behind his head. "I figured the good-night kiss *alone* would take hours."

Rusty and Wyatt giggled with unchecked hilarity.

Not about to be outmatched by Jake, Maggie breezed into the room. She bypassed the boys and headed straight for Jake, not stopping until she stood right in front of him. Her arms folded in front of her, she fastened her eyes on his and told him pointedly, "There was no good-night kiss. I didn't even show him the door—Harry did. Not that this is any of your business," Maggie concluded, so stiffly the boys giggled even more.

Jake stretched languorously and stood. Satisfaction gleamed in his dark eyes. "Sorry it didn't work out," he said smoothly.

Ha! "I just bet you are," Maggie murmured under her breath, so only he could hear.

Jake smiled and clasped her hand in a gentle yet implacable grip. "Guys, we're going down the hall to my room to talk," he announced matter-of-factly. "You stay here and watch the game, okay?"

"Okay, Unka Jake," the boys murmured sleepily, snuggling even farther into their covers.

Knowing Jake was right—they did need to talk— Maggie let Jake guide her into the master bedroom suite. A king-size bed, covered with a beige-black-and-gold paisley spread, dominated the spacious room. Matching drapes and coordinating miniblinds lined the windows. The walls and carpeted floor were also done in beige. It was purely a man's domain, uncluttered and comfortable, and it suited him perfectly.

But she wasn't here to admire his lair, she reminded herself bluntly. She was here to confront him about the purpose behind his actions this evening.

"Why did you do that?" she demanded, planting her hands on her hips.

Jake's eyes swept the length of her figure-hugging velvet dress. Once again, to her mounting frustration, he was the picture of innocence. "Do what?" he asked with comically exaggerated naivete.

"Make the boys suffer through a long boring dinner, just because you disapprove of my plans to find a husband."

"First, dinner wasn't all that long—only an hour and a half. It just seemed longer, 'cause you were so bored."

"And anyway," a youthful voice chimed in from Jake's open doorway, "we weren't sufferin', Maggie. We were just trying to look like we was."

"Were," Maggie corrected.

"Whatever," Rusty shrugged.

"We were really having a good time," Wyatt added reassuringly.

"You were throwing peas and peaches!" Maggie reprimanded. The twins might be young and mischievous, but she was certain they knew better than that. Her hunch was confirmed by the sheepish looks on their faces.

"Yeah, well, Unka Jake paid us to do that," Wyatt replied.

"He did what!" Maggie did a double take as Jake clamped a hand over his face and groaned and the two pajama-clad boys sauntered farther into the room. Both looked very glad to be the center of attention once again.

"He paid us to misbehave," Rusty explained.

"Yeah," Wyatt chimed in with a nod. "Two dollars each, all in quarters. He promised to take us to the video arcade tomorrow, so we can use them."

Maggie glared at Jake. This was really low, using the boys to ruin her husband hunt.

"Oh he did, did he?"

The boys nodded earnestly and then said, "You told us to do it, too, Maggie."

Maggie's jaw dropped. She protested heatedly. "I most certainly did not!" In fact, she had no idea where they even got that idea.

The twins continued to nod enthusiastically.

"Don't you remember?" Rusty prodded earnestly. "Before dinner, when you was helping us with our ties? You said to do exactly what Unka Jake said, so we did and we threw food, and at the end, after dessert, we roughhoused under the dining room table so he could get us and him outta there at a decent hour."

"He said it was a joke," Wyatt added helpfully, "to show you that Mac Malone was not the boyfriend for you." Beaming, Wyatt stuck out his chest and boasted proudly, "Unka Jake said we did a good job, too."

"A real good job," Rusty echoed happily.

"You know, boys, I think you've helped me out enough here," Jake drawled, not nearly as regretfully as Maggie would've liked to see him under the circumstances. "I think you better leave the rest of the explaining to me."

"Okay, Unka Jake." Wyatt smiled. "We're bored talkin' 'bout that, anyway. What we really came in to tell you was that the Rangers got another home run. Now they're ahead six to two."

"That's great." Jake smiled. "Now, how about I tuck you in one more time?"

"All right."

Before he could get them all the way out of the room, the twins paused in the portal. "Maggie, do we still get to do somethin' special tomorrow, like you promised?'' Rusty asked.

Maggie nodded. ''You boys lived up to your end of the bargain.'' Such as it was, anyway. She looked at Jake and announced with no small degree of satisfaction, ''Now it's my turn to live up to mine.''

## Chapter Seven

"They're finally asleep, thank God," Jake said, joining Maggie out by the pool, a little after 10:00 p.m.

She sighed wearily. "I'm glad to hear it."

Jake pulled up a chair and sat down beside her. He was glad to see she was still in the demure but sexy coffee-colored velvet dress she'd been wearing at dinner; he really liked the way she looked in that. He was not so happy to note she was apparently still mad as hell at him for his recently admitted shenanigans. Which doubtless explained her reason for sitting alone and brooding in the darkness of the Texas night, next to the shimmering blue of the lit pool.

"Still mad at me?"

Maggie turned her head. He'd never seen her more furious than she was at that instant.

"I'd have to care to be mad," she announced flatly.

"Ouch!" he said, in response to her insult. Already sorry about the way he'd behaved—Jake knew he never should have invited Mac Malone over in the first place—Jake winced.

She scooted her chair away from his with a screech

and continued in a voice that trembled with outrage. "You really are a rotten, scheming lowlife scum!"

Double ouch, Jake thought. On the other hand, he wasn't the only one in the wrong here, and the sooner Maggie realized that, the better. "So I made a point tonight." He moved his chair closer to hers again, so they could still argue intimately and their voices wouldn't carry. "So what?"

"And that point was what, Jake?" Maggie surged out of her chair. "That you couldn't pick a potential husband for me if you tried—which thus far, I might add, I don't think you have."

Jake stood. In an effort to help her calm down, he put his hands on her shoulders. "My point is, Maggie honey, that you can't script falling in love with someone. You can't make it happen. It either does or it doesn't. The time is either right or it isn't."

Maggie shrugged free of his light, easy grip. "Well, for your information, according to Sabrina, we all make our own destiny and according to my inner clock," Maggie fumed, stalking away from him, "the time is very right for me to marry and settle down."

Jake had no doubt that was true. Problem was, his inner clock wasn't telling him the same. So he did the only thing he could when talk got too intimate and too close to home. He changed the subject.

"Who the heck is Sabrina?" Jake demanded.

Maggie flushed and threw up her hands. For the umpteenth time since she had trespassed onto the Rollicking M, she looked sorry she had ever spoken. "Never mind who Sabrina is," she told him shortly.

Which in turn made him all the more curious. "Not so fast." He grabbed her before she could exit and hauled her close. "You can't throw something like that out and just walk away," he told her.

"I'd like to know why the heck not." Maggie poked him in the chest and tossed her head. "You do as much all the time, only telling me what you want me to know."

A mistake, Jake realized instantly. "So, set a good example and show me how it should be done," he coaxed softly. He didn't want Maggie to be a mystery to him.

Maggie sighed. "She's this fortune-teller I know."

"Fortune-teller," Jake echoed, astonished.

"See?" Maggie scowled at him. "I knew it was a mistake, confiding in you."

No, it wasn't, Jake thought. "Now, Maggie honey, don't be that way." In fact, confiding in him was the smartest thing she'd done so far. If not for him, she'd still be pursuing her ridiculously organized husband hunt full-time.

Desperate to make peace with her once again, Jake hooked an arm around her waist, sank into a chair and pulled her onto his lap, all in one smooth motion. When she tried to get up, he anchored her implacably. "I didn't mean to embarrass you," he confessed, brushing the hair from her cheek. "Honest." He placed a palm over his heart. "I was just surprised, is all."

Maggie continued glowering at him wordlessly and she did not uncross her arms, even when he tried to pry them loose.

"Please," Jake persuaded softly. "Tell me?"

"As much as I love to hear you beg," she deadpanned insincerely, "the answer is still and will continue to be no."

Jake noted that even though her arms were crossed tightly in a defensive position in front of her, she wasn't trying to get away from him anymore. He took solace in that. "Has Sabrina read the fortunes of your brothers and sisters, too?" he asked, stroking a hand lightly from her shoulder to her elbow.

Again, Maggie pulled her upper body away from him. "I don't have any sisters. Only brothers."

Now they were getting somewhere, Jake thought, glad that his oblique approach to finding out more about Maggie was working. "How old are they?" he asked curiously.

Maggie settled her bottom a little more squarely on his lap. "They're all younger."

With a great deal of effort, Jake ignored the delicious heat transferring from her curvy derriere to the front of his jeans. "Where are they?"

"They all live here in Texas," Maggie told him, her face glowing with familial pride. "Deke is a rancher in San Angelo, Billy is an ex-pro football player turned teacher and coach—he lives in Houston. And Frank is an Austin businessman."

Though she had answered his question, it was also clear to Jake that Maggie was working to keep a great deal of psychological distance between them. "What do your brothers think of this husband-hunting scheme of yours?" Jake asked.

Maggie shrugged and, relaxing a bit as she talked about her family, finally unclenched her arms. "They think I'm crazy, of course," she said with affection in her voice. "But they're all for me leaving the New York life behind and returning to my roots."

Jake gave that some thought. He could see Maggie with three younger brothers, all trying their damnedest to both protect her and talk some sense into her. "How come *they're* not trying to fix you up?"

Maggie's chin jutted out stubbornly. "'Cause I won't let them, that's why. I don't want them involved in my love life."

"Why not?" Jake asked. He'd bet they were involved in everything else. There'd been too much unchecked affection in her voice for them not to be.

"It'd be just too weird." Maggie sighed. Absently, she toyed with a button on his shirt as she explained, "I had to be both mom and dad to them after my parents died. So our relationship isn't the normal one between siblings, as I've always had to be the super-responsible one among us."

Jake thought of the sacrifices that must've required for her. The fact she hadn't resented having to make them only made him respect her all the more; she was one lady with a lot of heart and soul. "They must love you very much," he said softly, thinking how much his own two nephews already loved her after spending only two days with her.

Maggie's eyes grew liquid with happiness as she reflected on her family. "Yeah, we're close."

"That's nice. It's important to have family," Jake said. Briefly, he rested his face against the softness of her hair.

"Yes, it is."

Jake stroked her shoulder gently as he inhaled the floral scent of her shampoo. He drew back curiously.

"So, how did you ever get hooked up with a fortune-teller?" he asked.

Maggie grinned. Her blue eyes danced in a way that let him know she considered the fortune-telling to be pure fun. "You just won't give up, will you?" she teased.

"Not in this lifetime." Jake returned her smile playfully, then waited. As he had hoped, Maggie confided in him.

"I saw Sabrina for the first time when I was a kid. I was visiting my cousin Hallie in Chicago. She and I and a friend of ours, Clarissa, went to the SummerFest fair in Bridgeport every year. Sabrina had a tent set up there and she told our fortunes."

"What'd she predict for you?" Jake studied Maggie's face, realizing she was every bit as stunningly beautiful on the inside as she was on the outside.

Maggie smiled, a little shyly. "She told me I'd marry a cowboy."

*And not only am I a cowboy,* Jake mused, *but she keeps calling me 'cowboy', too.*

Aware Maggie would not be happy with anything less than true love, given and received, he asked, "So how come you're looking for millionaires then?" Why wasn't she out looking for *romance?*

Her head shot up. She regarded him with astonishment. "Because I'm wealthy. And I don't want anyone either marrying me for my money and success, or feeling inferior or upset because I do possess them."

That made a lot of sense. "Was that a problem with your ex-fiancé?" Jake asked softly.

Regretfully, Maggie nodded, and went back to playing with the buttons on his shirt. "I learned, during the fight we had when we broke up, that the thing that most attracted him to me was the fame and fortune. Naturally, that wasn't a pleasant surprise.''

"Naturally," Jake agreed, having a very good idea how much that must have hurt a tenderhearted woman like Maggie.

"And since I plan to live a rather low-key life from here on out," Maggie continued practically, "I didn't want that to be the case with anyone I marry. So I'm looking for someone not the least impressed with what I've done.''

"Someone who loves you for who you are in here," Jake touched the area above her heart.

Maggie nodded.

Their eyes met, held.

"You understand.''

And that pleased her, Jake noticed, very much.

"I've had to put up with the same, ever since I started making real money," Jake confessed. "Women who wouldn't look twice at me when I was a poor cowpoke now practically break their necks to let me know they're available and put themselves in my path.''

She grinned, realizing that he had unwittingly just described her, too. "Like me," she said.

"Oh, not quite like you," Jake drawled. No one was quite like Maggie.

Silence fell between them once again. Jake couldn't quite say how it was happening, but she was growing on him, breaking the self-imposed shell of isolation he'd built around himself years ago. Then, it had been the only way he could survive. Now, he was beginning to wonder if that had been the right path to take after all. Maybe he should let someone get a little bit close to him. Someone like Maggie.

He paused. "Did you mean what you said tonight at dinner about staying out of the public eye? Or were you just trying to let Mac know in a not-so-subtle way that you were not going to be his ticket to fame?"

"I meant it." Maggie released a beleaguered-sounding sigh. "I really am tired of being speculated about in the press. Heck, people don't even believe I'm really quitting modeling, if you believe the latest gossip in *Personalities!* magazine. They think it's all a giant publicity ploy."

"Isn't it?"

"No. I want out. I want a more normal life, with a husband and kids and family vacations and car pools and baseball games and trips to the supermarket. Despite all the advice to the contrary, I really am going to say goodbye to public life. And when people see the announcement of my marriage in the Houston newspaper—not on the society page but with all the other happy local couples—when they read I plan to concentrate on making a home for my husband and myself and our children from now on, that I intend to learn the business of ranching from the ground up, they'll know it's true."

What Maggie was describing was, unbeknownst to her, uncomfortably close to his life with Louellen. She, too, had been a homemaker and mother who shared his interest in the ranch. She, too, had valued family and their life together above all else. To the point she hadn't wanted to waste a second of it. What Maggie didn't know was that he couldn't go back to that. Couldn't take those kinds of risks. Not anymore.

Jake stiffened unhappily. Maggie swiftly followed suit.

Her hands on his shoulders, Maggie levered herself off his lap and stood. "Well, if it helps, Jake," she announced loftily, apparently mistaking the reasons behind his sudden wary silence, "I forgive you for tonight."

As much as Jake did not want to admit it, he knew he would sleep better, knowing she wasn't still mad at him. "How come?" he asked her curiously, as he rose, too.

Maggie shrugged as they stood face-to-face. "I wish to heck I knew."

They continued staring at each other. Though she was doing her best to hide it, he could've sworn he saw the same yearning reflected on her face, that he occasionally felt in his heart. The yearning to be close to someone, even if it was only for the moment this time, instead of forever.

He continued to study her. Loving the way she looked in the dress. Wishing he could see her without it.

As the seconds drew out, and their eyes continued to meet, her chest began to rise and fall rapidly, as if she'd just run a long distance. "Well," she said, a little faintly, backing away from him just a tad, "I better go on up and get some sleep. The boys will be up early and I did promise them something special tomorrow."

Jake remembered. "And I promised them a visit to the video arcade," he said.

"Right." She admonished him with a lift of her

brow. "So they can spend all those quarters you gave them for disrupting my date tonight."

He grinned sheepishly and since he could do nothing else, owned up to his deliberate mischief with an unrepentant grin.

"You are shameless," Maggie continued to admonish as she planted a fist on her hip.

"Yeah, well...what can I say?" Jake traced the compelling silhouette of her body beneath the clinging lines of her dress. He knew she wouldn't believe him if he told her he did not normally do things like this. "I was inspired," Jake confessed. The same way, he admitted recklessly, that he was inspired to do this. Giving in to an impulse that had been dogging him all night, he hooked an arm about her middle and dragged her closer.

"Jake, what are you doing?" Maggie demanded, flushing, though he was pretty sure that even as she asked she knew.

Jake also noted that although she'd laid her forearms across his chest, wedging distance between them, she wasn't resisting all that much, in fact hardly at all.

He cupped the back of her head with his hand, tilting her head up to his. "Giving you the good-night kiss you deserve," he said softly.

And then he did what he had wanted to do all evening, he covered her mouth with his. He gave her no quarter; to his stunned amazement, she gave him none back. It was all heat and passion, all deep, searing need. He wanted to consume her the way she was consuming him, and he nipped at her lips with his teeth, then dipped his head to kiss her throat, her collarbone. She moaned and collapsed against him. The trembling of her body was all the encouragement he needed. Tipping her head back and raking both hands through her hair, he lowered his lips to hers. He kissed her until they fought for breath, until she urged him on with her tongue. He kissed her with a sweetness and a tenderness he did not know he still possessed. And it was that vulnerability that made him pull away, in the end.

When he released her, he was as shaken as she apparently was, and no less dazed and confused. Which was no surprise, he figured, since he hadn't expected to feel like this again—if he had ever felt quite like this—any more than he had expected her to come into his life.

And that alone, was reason enough to stop. At least for tonight, he reasoned cooly.

He needed another day—*at least*—to think about what he was getting himself and her into here. To know if he would be able to cut his losses and move on as had become his habit. When she discovered, as did the others, that he could no longer love—not the way she needed or wanted anyway—when she discovered it just wasn't in him...not anymore...

"Well, good night," Maggie said softly.

Jake felt guilty, knowing she was privy to none of his thoughts, knowing she still felt there was a chance to have everything with him. He swallowed. Reined himself in. "Good night."

If he was any kind of gentleman, he told himself as she turned and walked away from him, he'd let her go now, before she got hurt any more. But he was no gentleman. And he hadn't been for some time.

Watching her walk back into the ranch house, Jake

knew no matter what happened that it would be a long time, if ever, before he forgot the gentle and loving way she had melted against him.

"MAGGIE, I'M TELLING YOU," Hallie said as they talked on the phone early the next morning before the boys got up. "It's a mistake to get involved with a bad boy, and that goes double when it's with a bad boy you know is not going to marry you!"

"Are we talking about me or you?" Maggie asked, aware the two of them had been so busy catching up on the men in their lives she hadn't had time to tell her about Sabrina yet.

"Both."

"So bad-boy Cody Brock is giving you a hard time, now that he's back in the house next door," Maggie surmised, able to tell Hallie still had a king-size crush on him.

"Not the way you think. Not the way he used to," Hallie replied, a bit too defensively.

"Then why do I hear that undercurrent of worry in your voice?"

"Because even though Cody seems to be a lot nicer and more successful now than I ever thought he would be when he finally grew up, he still hasn't been over his wild streak all that long," Hallie confessed with a troubled sigh.

Which meant what, exactly, Maggie wondered, as her worry over her cousin increased. "You're talking in riddles, Hallie."

Another silence, this more telling than the last. A sigh. A low, anguished wail. "Oh, Maggie," Hallie blurted out, sounding more upset than Maggie had ever heard her. "Cody's life is a wreck right now. He has a baby girl named Amy."

"Is he married?"

"No. And, for the moment, anyway, he has sole custody." Hallie paused, then confided reluctantly. "It's a long story."

Maggie just bet it was. "And you're in the middle of this?" Maggie asked her cousin, amazed. Somehow, she would have expected Hallie to run in the other direction, considering how relentlessly Hallie guarded her heart.

"Oh, Maggie, I can't help but be in the middle of it all," Hallie confided with another long, heartfelt sigh. "Cody means well but he doesn't know anything about taking care of babies."

"Meanwhile, you've come to his rescue," Maggie concluded, hoping this was not as big a mistake as it sounded.

"And then some," Hallie confirmed.

Another silence fell.

"But not to worry, Maggie," Hallie continued with a steadiness of purpose that was absolutely enviable. "I am still set on marrying someone sensible and dependable, like my banker friend, Tim Levine. And I think you should do so, too." In the background, a doorbell sounded. "Maggie, can you hang on a minute?" Hallie asked. "I want to see who that is."

"No problem," Maggie said, reminded she still hadn't told Hallie about Sabrina.

There was a low murmur of excited voices. A lot of static and noise on the other end as Hallie picked up the phone again. "Maggie, Cody's here. I've got to go. I'll call you back later, and if not tonight, then as soon as I can.'' She hung up the phone before Maggie could get a word in edgewise. Maggie stood holding the receiver.

Belatedly, she realized she had no clue if Hallie had seen Sabrina, too.

"I AM STILL SET on marrying someone sensible and dependable...and I think you should do so, too.'' Hallie's commonsense words were still ringing in Maggie's head as she went to the kitchen for breakfast.

An extralong dish towel tied apron-style around his ample waist, Harry was busy plating eggs and bacon to Jake and the boys. The boys, looking ready for action, had their stacks of quarters next to their plates.

"When does the arcade open?'' Maggie asked, sitting with them. She accepted the plate Harry handed her.

"We're in luck.'' Jake poured her some coffee. "I know one that is open twenty-four hours a day.''

"Yeah,'' Rusty enthused, shoveling eggs into his mouth with more than usual gusto. "Unka Jake said we could get goin' as soon as we finished eatin'.''

"Yep, he says no sense putting off 'til later what you can do right now,'' Wyatt parroted.

Did that include loving her, too? Maggie wondered uncertainly as she recalled their unbearably passionate, unexpectedly tender good-night kiss of the evening before. Much more of that and she might end up falling in love with him. This, when she knew for a fact that he had no desire for anything with her but a hot, passionate affair.

Unless he changed his mind...

If he changed his mind...

Oh, who was she kidding, Maggie scolded herself silently as she turned her attention to her breakfast. The odds were that was not going to happen. Jake was interested in pleasure and fun, not children and a long-term commitment.

She couldn't let herself fall into that trap. And the only way to ensure that from happening was to put the barriers up between them and continue her search.

"HOT DOG, Unka Jake! I really kaboomed the heck out of that one!" Rusty said.

"Can I try next?" Wyatt asked, tugging on his sleeve.

Jake nodded. The two boys went to it, Rusty watching raptly and shouting encouragement as Wyatt played the game. Beside him, Maggie was strangely quiet as she had been all morning, which was odd, Jake thought, considering the way the previous evening had ended. He thought she had enjoyed their kisses as much as he had. He'd thought he was the only one harboring doubts about the wisdom of beginning a hot, tempestuous love affair.

"Do you still have your headache?" he asked, above the constant noise of the video arcade. She looked as though something was wrong.

Maggie shook her head. She took his arm and drew him to a deserted corner, where they could still keep a good eye on the boys. "No. I was wondering though—" She stopped before she could finish and drew a tremulous breath.

"What?" Jake asked.

"Who are you going to fix me up with next?"

Jake couldn't have been more stunned and hurt had he taken a poison arrow to the heart.

"I mean, you did promise," Maggie rushed on, her cheeks pinkening with what he could only figure as embarrassment at having to ask him to help her find suitable dates. "And you struck me as the kind of man who keeps his promises," she finished succinctly.

He did keep his promises, Jake thought irritably. And he had promised himself he wouldn't get involved with this husband-hungry wench from the very beginning. So if he'd had his feelings hurt here—and he admitted to himself they were a tad injured—he had only himself to blame.

Aware she was waiting on an answer and that his patience as a matchmaker, even in jest, was exhausted, Jake replied vaguely, "I'm still thinking on it, Maggie, honey."

Why was he angry when he'd known all along what she was after? Jake patted her on the shoulder and in an effort to lighten the moment, said, "I want the next one to be perfect for you."

Maggie was silent, studying his face. "No more jokes?"

Jake admitted he was tempted, but he also knew continuing to tease her was a mistake. It always ended up with the two of them feeling even closer. And closer was something they were obviously not destined to be.

He shook his head. His expression became serious. His mood reluctant. "No more jokes," he said quietly, meeting and holding her eyes. It was time they faced the truth; considering what they each wanted and expected to get out of life, the two of them were and always would be all wrong for each other. "The next one, Maggie, will be for real," he promised.

"When?" Whatever she was thinking, was a mystery to him.

Jake paused, knowing if he was going to do right by her this time that it would take some time. "A few days?" he suggested optimistically. Maybe by then his sister Kelsey would be back, and he could send Maggie off on her date and on her way.

One thing was certain. He couldn't stand seeing her with other men, not feeling the way he did. Because like it or not, he wanted to make Maggie his in the most intimate, elemental way. And he had a disturbing hunch that was a feeling that was just not going to go away.

# Chapter Eight

"I think you've caught quite enough fireflies for one evening, boys."

"Awww, Maggie!" Wyatt stamped his foot.

"Please!" Rusty begged.

Maggie held up a hand stop-sign fashion. "No wheeling and dealing tonight, guys. It's past your bedtime already. You need to free your fireflies—so they can continue to enjoy nature—and then get upstairs, hit the shower and get that Crazy String washed out of your hair."

The twins studied her, looking for a way to delay the inevitable bedtime. "If we cooperate, will you read us a story?" Wyatt finally asked slyly.

"A short one," Maggie promised. She handed over the plastic jar holding their cache of fireflies. "Take the lid off and say goodbye to your fireflies."

Wyatt and Rusty stared at the fireflies solemnly. "Goodbye," they yelled. Rusty unscrewed the hole-studded metal lid. They all three watched as the ten fireflies they'd caught took off, their bodies winking red in the darkness of the summer evening.

"You missed our fireflies, Unka Jake," Wyatt said,

as Jake came outside to join them, portable phone in hand.

"I'll be sure to catch them next time then," Jake said, affectionately ruffling Wyatt's then Rusty's hair. He lifted his hand away. "Yuk. What did you guys get in your hair? It's all sticky."

"Maggie bought us some Crazy String."

Jake looked baffled.

Maggie explained, "It comes in a can, and sprays out like string. You have fights with it. It's harmless fun. We'd show you but we're all out of string."

"Hmmm." Jake nodded. He had been on the phone most of the afternoon and evening, talking nonstop to business associates. He'd been so busy, in fact, he hadn't even joined them for dinner.

"I was getting ready to take the boys up to shower now," Maggie said to Jake, telling herself not to be disappointed that Jake seemed to be avoiding her like the plague.

"I'll do that," Jake volunteered.

Maggie paused. Jake had been distant toward her since she had reminded him of his promise to introduce her to eligible wealthy men. "Are you sure?" she asked.

"Positive." He looked at the baseball mitts, soccer balls and practice goal, and assorted riding toys scattered across the lawn. "If you'll gather up the toys and stuff down here, and put them away, I'll supervise the showers," he offered.

Maggie knew, as hyperactive as the boys were, that this was more of an undertaking than Jake seemed to realize. Hence, she was tempted to offer to help him on that score, too. On the other hand, maybe it would be better for her and Jake to spend as much time as possible apart. If they were apart there could be no more fighting, no more tension, no more unexpectedly intimate talk or kissing. Maybe this was a blessing in disguise after all.

Maggie met his eyes. "You've got yourself a deal," she said.

MAGGIE HEARD the shrieks of youthful laughter and thundering footsteps from all the way downstairs. Harry Wholesome sighed, rolling his eyes, as he set the tall glass of mint tea he'd brought for Maggie beside her. "I don't even want to imagine what those rascals are up to now," he said.

"Not to worry, Harry. I'll go see what's going on," Maggie soothed as she put the evening paper aside.

"But you just sat down," Harry protested. "And you've been entertaining those boys all day long."

"It's okay." Maggie smiled wearily at Jake's housekeeper. "I had to go up in a minute anyway. I promised to read the boys a bedtime story as soon as they'd finished their showers." From the sound of those footsteps, Maggie was sure Rusty and Wyatt were no longer in the shower.

But they should have been, Maggie decided, a scant minute and a half later, barely able to believe the mischief the two boys had gotten into in less than fifteen minutes. Stark naked, dripping water, soap and shampoo, they were chasing each other around upstairs.

Knowing the roughhousing and mess making had to stop immediately, Maggie put two fingers in her mouth and whistled loud enough to stop a New York cab half a block away. "Freeze right where you are!"

she ordered, efficiently handing them both a towel to wrap up in. As soon as they had, she demanded, "Where's your Uncle Jake?"

Wyatt flicked the bubbles out of his eyes. "Dunno," he said.

"Yes, we do," Rusty corrected, looking with fascination at the soapy water puddling on the carpet beneath his feet. "He's talking bizness on the phone whiles we get our shampoos," Wyatt said.

"Oh, yeah," Wyatt said. "He had to go in the other room 'cause he couldn't hear, we was making so much noise."

Meanwhile, the bathroom shower in his bedroom was still running full blast. "Okay, guys, let's go rinse you off, and get you in your pj's," Maggie said. She'd deal with Jake later. Boy, would she deal with Jake.

Within ten minutes Wyatt and Rusty were ensconced in their beds. "No story, hmm?" Wyatt guessed sadly.

Maggie shook her head. "Nope," she said, as disappointed as the boys about that, as she enjoyed reading to them very much. "You guys lost that privilege when you started your water fight," she told them firmly.

"We're sorry, Maggie," Rusty said around a heartfelt yawn. "Guess we got carried away, using the baby shampoo like Crazy String."

"Yeah, sorry Maggie," Wyatt apologized, continuing to look very sad and lonely all of a sudden.

Realizing all they'd been through, in being dumped on Jake's doorstep while their mom set out after their runaway father, Maggie couldn't help but feel for them, and some of her exasperation began to fade.

"Listen, guys, you have to do a better job of behaving," she told them quietly, bending to kiss them good-night and tuck them in, in turn. "'Cause I know that you know better than to make the kind of mess you made tonight."

Neither disputed her assessment of the situation. A thoughtful silence ensued. "Are we grounded?" Wyatt asked eventually.

Maggie realized they expected to be. She nodded. "Yes. I'm afraid so, guys. No television the rest of today and all day tomorrow."

Sighing, they accepted their punishment in stride. She kissed them again, noting they were already half asleep—no surprise, since it was after 10:00 p.m.— and headed out the door.

She still had one heck of a mess to clean up, and one very irresponsible cowboy to chasten. And this one, unlike his nephews, she determined furiously, was not going to be let off so easy.

JAKE FOLLOWED the wet footprints in the carpet all the way into the master bedroom, and the adjoining bath suite, complete with sunken whirlpool tub, separate glass shower stall, twin sinks, and sit-down vanity.

Maggie was on her hands and knees, sopping up water with a stack of towels. She did not look happy to see him as she sat back on her heels and snapped, "Your business finished?"

"Actually, no," Jake replied. He hunkered down beside her and, picking up a towel, began blotting the puddles of water on the ceramic tile floor. He didn't need to see the glimmering resentment in her deep blue eyes to know he was in trouble. Big trouble.

"What happened here?" he asked curiously. It looked like the aftermath of an explosion of water and bubbles.

"What happened here or what should have happened here?" Maggie asked as she wiped a streak of foamy white suds off the side of the tub.

Jake winced at the asperity in her tone. "I told the boys to get their showers while I made a quick call. Don't look at me like that. It isn't anything they haven't done before. I turn on the water and adjust the temperature. They hop in, shampoo their hair and wash with soap, rinse and get back out."

Maggie regarded him with a disbelieving smirk. "Well, they did all of the above and more."

Jake paused, aware his heart had taken on a slow and heavy beat. "Was that what that racket was?"

"Yes." Maggie slapped a towel on the floor and surged to her feet.

Knowing they were on the verge of a showdown, he followed her lead.

Her cute chin tilted at him pugnaciously, she placed her hands on her slender hips and squared off with him like a gunfighter at the OK Corral. "If you heard all that, why didn't you come and see what was going on?" she demanded.

Jake frowned. He hadn't misbehaved here, his nephews had, and he was damned if he was going to take the blame for it. "Because I was in the middle of a conversation. One that was critical to my business."

"Right." Her mood still sharply disapproving, she shoved a towel at his middle. "Well, now that you're done with your critical business, you can finish this." She started to step by him.

Jake's jaw dropped in stunned amazement as he studied the riot of color sweeping into her cheeks. "You're leaving this to me?"

Spine stiff, Maggie flashed him a lofty smile and marched past him. "Neither Harry nor I should have to do it since you were the one responsible for supervising their showers tonight," she said sweetly.

Not about to let this deteriorate into an all-out war between them, Jake caught her arm as she passed and dragged her back to face him. "What burr is under your saddle?" he demanded, irated.

She narrowed her eyes at him smugly. "As if you don't know!"

"I don't!" Jake said in utter frustration.

Maggie merely folded her arms in front of her and faced him in stormy silence.

"So I screwed up—" Jake said, after a moment, dropping his grip on her arm.

"You seem to do that a lot," Maggie agreed. "Especially when it comes to people and commitments."

"Excuse me?"

Leaning closer, she spelled it out for him. "You don't have any problem committing yourself to a business deal or this ranch, but when it comes to hands-on responsibility to another person or family, you're not really the person to count on, are you?"

She'd hit the nail on the head, more than she knew. Jake had been running from closeness with others for years now. And unable to bear the thought of getting hurt again the way he had been, he was still running.

"You should have stayed with those boys, Jake," Maggie continued. "Just like you should be taking care of them, at least the majority of the time when you are home, instead of shifting the responsibility to Harry and me."

Jake swallowed. Much as he was loath to admit it, he knew that was true, too. He had kept his emotional distance from everyone, including his sister Kelsey, since he'd lost Louellen. It didn't mean he didn't love Kelsey and her boys, and maybe in a way, even her husband Clint. It did mean he couldn't confide in them, couldn't spend time with them. Couldn't let himself come to count on their continued presence in his life.

But Maggie didn't need to know that. She'd dissed him enough already.

Uncomfortable talking about himself, he steered the subject back to the problem at hand. "What exactly were Wyatt and Rusty doing in here tonight?"

"They were having a shampoo fight with their baby shampoo. They were smearing it all over each other."

Jake regarded the half dozen aerosol cans of baby shampoo scattered around them. "Sort of like they did with that Crazy String you bought 'em."

Maggie continued restlessly tapping her sneaker-clad foot. "Right. What were they doing with six cans of For Kids Only shampoo anyway?"

Jake regarded Maggie meditatively and tried not to notice the way her damp khaki walking shorts and cropped T-shirt were clinging to her. Or the fact there was a smear of soap just below her ribs. "There was a two-for-one sale on it earlier in the week. Harry knew it was the kind Kelsey liked to use on the boys, so he bought half a dozen cans and stuck them in the cabinet under the sink. Of course, Harry didn't antic-ipate the boys doing this, and neither did I."

Jake picked up one of the cans, shook it, pressed the dispenser and watched a ball of foamy mousse shampoo fill his palm. "But then, that was also before they had learned the joys of Crazy String," he said with mock solemnness.

"Wait a minute. You're blaming me for this?" Maggie asked, incredulous.

Jake shrugged. He was tempted to take the mischief his nephews had started one step further, if for no other reason than to give Maggie a way to use up all the adrenaline that was obviously coursing through her veins. "Makes about as much sense as you blaming me for something they thought of and did all on their own," he drawled. "Not that I'm disparaging my nephews entirely, you understand. I can see how this would be fun to smear on someone else." Demonstrating what he meant, Jake smeared the ball of shampoo down one side of Maggie's face, then the other.

Her cheeks, already pink, grew even pinker.

She scraped the shampoo off her cheeks and flung it to the floor. To his disappointment, she was clearly not amused.

"I am not going to play this game with you," she said stiffly.

"Sure?" Jake taunted with a smile. He filled his palm with another ball of mousse. Before she could dart safely out of reach, he smoothed a big gob of shampoo onto her golden hair. Then, for emphasis, worked it in.

Maggie drew a very deep, very long breath. The movement lifted her breasts beneath the clinging fabric of her cropped T-shirt. "Jake MacIntyre, I am warning you, this is a fight you do not want to start with me."

Judging by the excited glitter in her blue eyes, she was wrong about that, too.

"It isn't?" Jake took a third gob of shampoo and, slipping his hand beneath the hem of her T-shirt, smeared it across her bare midriff and into her warm, silky skin. "'Cause I gotta tell you, Maggie, it feels very right to me."

Her gaze remained stern and uncompromising but her stomach muscles quivered sensually beneath his questing hand. "Put the can down, right now," she ordered.

Jake shook his head slowly, never taking his eyes from hers. "I don't think I can do that," he teased playfully, as he continued to rub the shampoo into her trembling middle. "Not when there's so much shampoo left and so little time."

The next thing Jake knew, Maggie had picked up a can herself. She had aimed it straight at his collarbone, not stopping until she had filled the open V of his blue chambray work shirt with puffy white foam. Finished, she covered the foam with his shirt collar and smeared it in with the flat of her hand.

"Feel better?" she asked brightly, her eyes still holding his cheekily. "'Cause I know I do."

*No, but he was about to.* Jake grinned, inverted the can, pulled her cropped T-shirt out by the neck and sprayed a generous amount of foam in the direction of her breasts. The only sound from Maggie was the sharp intake of her breath.

Knowing it had become a contest of wills between them, to see who could keep from losing it the longest, he kept going until the can hissed, announcing it empty. Still smiling, he set the can aside with a gentle thud, returned his hand to her chest, and proceeded to run his hand across her front, smearing the shampoo between her shirt and skin, until her chest rose and fell with the sudden ragged intake of her breath and her nipples pressed urgently against the heel of his hand.

Swearing in a decidedly unladylike manner, she plucked his hand from her chest and pushed it away. "You are going to be sorry about that," she told him slowly and deliberately, still holding his gaze.

Able to see where this was going, Jake grabbed his jeans by the waist, and pulled them out an inch or so, giving her ample access to the most intimate part of him. "You want to spray me?" he taunted. "Spray away."

Maggie regarded him with scathing amusement, knowing he was taking this one-upmanship to new heights. "You don't think I'll do it, do you?" she demanded, giving him a censuring look.

Jake shrugged indifferently. "Considering that wherever the shampoo goes, your hand is going to go, too...no, Maggie, I don't." She wouldn't dare.

"Well, then, you're wrong." Her expression defiant, she filled the front of his jeans with mousse shampoo, continuing until the can hissed and sputtered.

Finished, she put the empty can aside, pushed the front of his jeans against his skin, and with the heel of her hand worked it in, in the same way he had worked it in across her breasts.

Jake didn't know which was more exciting, the pressure of her hand, or the gasp of dismay... excitement...when she discovered, quite inadvertently, what her actions had wrought. He was hard as a rock, and bound to get harder still before this was all over.

Looking more than a little disconcerted by what she'd so sensually discovered, Maggie stepped back, cheeks flaming. "Now that we're even—" she said.

"Whoa." Flattening his hands on either side of her, he caged her in his arms, and backed her up against the side of the glass-walled shower stall. "Where do you think you're going?"

Maggie twisted in his arms, trying in vain to propel herself in the direction of the door. "To wash this off, that's where."

"And drip it all over the carpet, so someone'll have to clean it up?" Jake asked, parroting her earlier— albeit justified—complaint. He shook his head. "I don't think so, Maggie."

"What are you planning?"

Mischief surged through him, completely unchecked by the cool warning in her wide blue eyes. "That we rinse off right here."

Maggie's breath hitched in her chest. "Jake, no—" she protested.

Too late, he had already moved her slightly to the side, and backed her into the ceramic-walled shower stall. Switched on the water. Pulled her underneath the warm, invigorating spray. "Damn you—" she sputtered, even as he dragged her against him and positioned them length to length.

"That's right," Jake muttered back, knowing—as she did—this reckoning had been coming from the first moment they had met and clashed. "Damn us both," he whispered.

Then his lips met hers, and all was lost in the sweet,

tender glory of the kiss. He expected her to fight him, not surge against him wildly. He expected her to cry foul, not to drag him even closer. But drag him closer she did, burying her hands in his hair, and opening her mouth to his. She kissed him fiercely. Avidly. Until the once-familiar surge of need came rushing through him. Until all the walls he had erected around him to keep the hurt at bay came tumbling down, and he was reaching for her, too, not with just his body, but with all his heart and soul.

MAGGIE HAD NOT expected any of this, but she couldn't fight it, either, not when the mere touch of his lips to hers, the soft brush of his dark mustache, and sweeping urgency of his tongue sent ripples of desire flowing through her in undulating waves. Longing swept through her as she boldly met him kiss for kiss, until she was aching and filled with a need unlike anything she had ever felt before. And still the water sluiced down on both of them, warmly drenching their clothes, taking all pretense of modesty away. Like it or not, Maggie thought, feeling him grow rock-hard against her, he made her want as fiercely as he did. He made her react, with everything that was feisty and feminine within her.

"Maggie—" he whispered her name as her knees gave way and she collapsed weakly against the tile wall. Her clothes clung to her body, her soaked T-shirt clearly outlined her throbbing breasts. And they were only just getting started, she knew.

"Maggie, I want to touch you." His mouth moved on hers effortlessly, demandingly, taking complete control of the kiss with ease.

Maggie groaned, knowing she wanted him to touch her, too. "Now you ask permission," she lamented with playful abandon, knowing he had already made her feel every bit as wild and reckless in affairs of the heart as he was.

"Tell me you want to touch me, too." His low voice burned with a quiet urgency that had nothing to do with ego and everything to do with desire. He positioned her toward the spray and rinsed off the fragrant shampoo they'd smeared all over each other.

"Oh, Jake," Maggie sighed and shut her eyes, as his hands swept the last of the bubbles away. With his gentle ministrations, the way he was turning her back around to face him, he was tempting her to believe this incredible feeling inside her was real, that theirs was a love that could actually be....

"Say it, Maggie," he commanded gruffly, still holding her close as he fit his lips over hers once again.

His arms were sure and strong, his kiss soft and warm and oh, so tempting. Maggie sighed again as his persuasive kiss came to a halt, every ardent sense in her aroused by his unwavering determination to make her his. There was no sense denying this was so, not when he already knew the truth.

"I want to touch you, too," she confessed with a soft ragged breath, washing away the soap on him, too. Maybe such close contact with each other would even help, she reasoned innocently enough. After all, what could it hurt? she wondered. Just one touch, intimately given, intimately received...

"Then show me, Maggie." Holding her close, he

pressed a kiss into her hair as the last of the shampoo on them was sluiced away by the shower.

*Stop it, Maggie. Stop it now, before it goes any further.* Maggie paused and raked her teeth across her lower lip. "Jake, I—" She tried to find the words that would put an end to the outrageous pleasure and predictably came up with zilch. Meanwhile, Jake was very busy, kissing her temples, her eyes, her nose and, finally, her mouth. Especially, Maggie thought with another languorous sigh, her mouth.

"Show me how much you want to touch me," he urged seductively, when her entire insides had gone soft as butter.

Feeling wicked under his spell, she unbuttoned his drenched shirt, parted the edges of the fabric and pushed them aside. Her palms slid over the silky damp mat of hair, and the smooth warm muscles beneath. He shuddered at her touch. She liked his response so much, she explored his flat male nipples with her fingertips until he groaned.

"My turn." Hands cupped around her waist, he turned them both so his back was to the wall, and the water sluiced down on their sides. His hands slid under her waist, beneath the hem of her cropped T-shirt, over her ribs, to her breasts. One quick motion, and her lacy bra was unsnapped. Before she could do more than draw a gasp of delight, her breasts fell free.

He cupped the weight of them in his hands, with infinite slowness brushed his thumbs across the tips. Once, and then again, and again and again. Nothing had ever felt so wonderful. Maggie moaned as her nipples budded tightly and fire swept through her middle, pooling low.

Not content with tactile exploration, Jake lifted the hem of her T-shirt and bared her breasts to his rapacious view. Hands cupped around her rib cage, holding her apart from him, he bent his head and circled the pale pink aureole of her breast with his tongue. Brushed it with his mustache. Then suckled her tenderly again. When her knees weakened treacherously and she thought she could stand it no more, he turned his attention to her other breast and did the same.

Lightning zigzagged through her, further destroying her resolve not to become involved with this wild cowboy. Aware she'd never experienced anything sweeter or more erotic, Maggie cupped his head with both her hands. Darn his mischievous soul, he made her want…so much more than she had ever dreamed possible.

He smiled at the restless way she trembled, looking as if he had always known they would end up this way. And somewhere deep inside Maggie, she had known it, too.

"Again?" he asked softly, dutifully returning his attention to her other breast, caressing and suckling at will, over and over, until at last she went wild, moaning impatiently and arching against him.

"Or perhaps you want this—" Jake suggested sensually. Pushing her back against the wall, he divested her of her shirt and bra, tossed her clothing aside and dropped to his knees. Unsnapped and unzipped her shorts. Cupped his hands in the waistband of her shorts and slid them down to midthigh. Thumbs slipping beneath the elastic of her bikini panties, he kissed the golden nest of curls through the transparent wisp of ecru lace.

Maggie shifted positions with a mixture of anticipation and desire, even as she lovingly whispered his name. "Jake—"

"You're right." He grinned. "I guess I better dispense with these, too."

Thanks to some quick action on his part, her delicate panties went the way of her shorts. With the expertise of a born seducer, his hand slid between her thighs and he parted her legs the few inches the shorts would allow. Maggie moaned as his fingers found her first, then his lips. Then his hands again. She lifted herself against him, pleading for a more intimate union, aware even as she moaned that she was on the brink. And then his mouth was on her again, in the most intimate of kisses, and she was gone. Floating. Free.

A SATISFACTION DEEPER than any he had ever known coursed through him, Jake held Maggie until she stopped trembling, then stood. Cupping the silken warmth of her rounded buttocks in both hands, he began to think about his own needs as he brought her against him.

Her blue eyes so misty with pleasure, Maggie gazed up at him. He looked into her eyes and the depth of her yearning shook him to his soul. He didn't want to be involved, not the way she wanted, but he feared he already was.

"My turn?" she whispered shakily, already reaching complaisantly for the zipper on his jeans.

Jake nodded.

As a lover Maggie was both far more innocent and sexier than he had imagined her to be. Guilt and regret flowed through him. He was going to have to be careful not to hurt her, to let her down easy when their impetuous affair ended.

"Like this?" Maggie asked.

He tensed as her warm soft hands closed around him, then trembled on the edge of release, as her bare breasts brushed against him.

"Or like this?" she queried softly, stroking him tip to base then circling gently.

Much more of this and he knew he really would explode in her hands, instead of deep inside her, where he desperately needed to be. But first, reluctant as he might be to consider them, there were essentials that had to be taken care of.

"Protection," Jake rasped impatiently in her ear, as he struggled to retain control of a situation that was desperately close to becoming unmanageable in the way only a hot, passionate love affair could be.

"Do you have any here with you, Maggie?" Jake asked.

Maggie blinked, stunned.

"Are you using any contraception?" he asked gently, afraid he already knew the answer to that, just by the stricken way she was looking at him. "Because, if not..." he let the thought trail off, knowing enough had been said. Damn it all, he disparaged himself silently, he should have thought of this earlier, should have made a run to the store, but he hadn't, so it was his fault they were not going to be able to progress to the next stage of lovemaking.

"No. I'm not on the Pill and I don't have a diaphragm or anything," Maggie admitted. "Nor do I have anything for you."

"So much for that then," Jake said grimly, turning off the shower with a swift jerk of the knob. He sighed heavily and could not have looked more disappointed. "As much as I want to be inside you tonight, it's not worth the risk of you getting pregnant. Like it or not, Maggie, we'll just have to wait."

ALTHOUGH MAGGIE doubted it was his intention, Jake couldn't have cooled her ardor any more effectively had he thrown a bucket of ice water on her.

And it was not just because she would have preferred not to have anything synthetic between them when they did finally consummate their passion, Maggie realized, stunned. It was because at that moment tonight, when all the barriers between them had come down, when she had given herself to him unreservedly, and they had been on the verge of making wild, wonderful, magnificent love, she had wanted nothing more than for Jake to father any children she might have—whether they ever married or not! But he did not want that; he couldn't have made that more clear. And that, in turn, dictated what she had to do. Like it or not, she told herself, ignoring the sizzling aftershocks still coursing through her body, she had to call an end to this madness, and go back to her original plan.

"But there are other ways of pleasuring each other," Jake continued, beginning to cheer up slightly as he reached for her again.

"No, Jake." Hands up in a halting gesture, Maggie pushed him away. There was no way she could pretend this discussion hadn't happened and simply pick up where they had left off, on the brink of soul-shattering ecstasy. "No."

His hands stilled. He was silent a long moment. Dazed, almost. Which was, as it happened, Maggie thought furiously, almost exactly the way she felt. Who said turnabout wasn't fair play?

"No?" he finally said, stepping away from her.

"No," Maggie repeated, even more firmly, aware she was so frustrated and disappointed at having their impetuous tryst cut short she was on the verge of bursting into tears.

Yanking her shorts up, grabbing her T-shirt and bra, she pushed by him. She wasn't sure who she was more disappointed in, him or herself. Because, darn it all, she scolded herself emotionally, she knew better than to get involved with someone who couldn't, wouldn't, give her what she wanted and needed most. "We shouldn't have started this," she told him firmly. Especially since she knew he was not the least bit interested in marriage.

He grabbed her arm and swung her around to face him, the silkiness of her breasts collided with the hair-whorled musculature of his chest. "Correction, Maggie," he said as the warmth of his skin brushed hers with sizzling and undeniable intensity. "We shouldn't have stopped."

"Excuse me?"

"Look, I agree that a monkey wrench has been thrown into our plans and that a discussion of contraception devices is uncomfortable, but the bottom line is we don't have to let the evening end this way."

Unable to hide the hurt and confusion his attitude had caused her, Maggie stepped back. "Don't we?"

she countered cooly. "I want to be *married,* Jake. I want children."

"I know that," he said simply, as if he had accepted that about her, even though he did not feel the same. His expression gentled. "It doesn't change the way I feel about you."

But it should, Maggie thought desperately. "But marriage and a family are not what you want, right?" she asked, troubled, as she hurriedly pulled on first her soaked bra and then her shirt.

Jake raked his hands through his hair. "I've told you that's not in the cards for me," he said roughly, making no apology for that fact. "I'm not father material, Maggie. Not even close."

"How do you know?"

"Because of the way I screwed up with the twins tonight. Because of—" He stopped himself abruptly.

"What?" Maggie prodded him impatiently, when he didn't continue.

"Nothing," Jake cut off her questions with a brusque look. "It's just obvious in a lot of ways," he argued emotionally, before taking her in his arms once again. Ignoring the resisting stiffness of her body, he clamped one hand around her waist and used the other to smooth the silky blond hair away from her face. "But that doesn't stop me from wanting you or you from wanting me, or us from belonging together, at least temporarily." He gave her a look, reminding her of the heat and fire of their tryst. "We're going to make love eventually, Maggie. I know it in here." He pointed to his chest. "And in here." He pointed to his head.

As much as she was loath to admit it, Maggie feared

that was true. He had only to kiss her, for her resistance to scatter like leaves in the wind.

"So why not continue what we started, as much as we are able, now—tonight?" Jake persisted amiably, still smoothing her hair away from her cheek. "At the very least we could cuddle and kiss and fool around a little more in my bed. If you want—" his voice dropped another seductive notch "—you could even sleep in there tonight."

"No," Maggie retorted, just as sincerely, "we can't."

"Why not?" Though she was being uncooperative, Jake didn't look ready to give up any time soon.

"Because it's not right," she insisted stubbornly, feeling her heart begin to break, as she realized that in all probability Sabrina had been wrong, Maggie was not destined to be with Jake after all.

"Because you're not offering me what I want. Not long-term. You may be made for hot passionate affairs, Jake, but I'm not," she told him stormily. "I'm a married 'til I die kind of woman, and I always will be." And darn it all, she was not going to apologize for that!

"Meaning what?" Jake demanded, his resentment of her determination to stick by her plan to find her own Mr. Right, come hell or high water, beginning to show. "That you're still on the great husband hunt and you won't let yourself be distracted, even for something as great as what we just shared?" he questioned angrily.

Maggie folded her arms in front of her and held her ground. Knowing it was time he accepted some things, too, she told him seriously, "Look, Jake, whether you help me or not, I am going to find the man who was meant for me and me alone. And when I do, I'm going to do whatever it takes to make him mine. Not just for today or tomorrow, but for all eternity. And no one, not even you, is going to stop me!''

## Chapter Nine

"Did Jake leave already?" Maggie asked Harry, early the following morning. The storm that had started shortly after midnight showed no sign of abating. Rain pounded torrentially against the roof of the breakfast nook, and blurred the view of the backyard.

Harry nodded as he lifted fluffy, golden flapjacks onto a plate. "He was out of here at the crack of dawn."

And it had been raining hard most of the night, Maggie knew. She hated to think about Jake driving in such a downpour. "Did he say when he'd be back?" she asked casually, as she poured herself a cup of coffee.

Harry shook his head. "He just said he had business in Houston and he would be back whenever it was done." Harry paused to give her an intent look. "The two of you have words or something last night?"

Maggie lifted the cup of coffee to her lips. "Why would you think that?" she inquired.

"He was in a terrible mood. The foulest I've seen since— Well, a long time."

He'd had good reason to be in a foul mood, Maggie

thought. The near-lovemaking had been upsetting to her as well. She was dangerously close to falling in love with Jake. And he couldn't have been more wrong for her. Doubtless, he was feeling the same misgivings about their increasing emotional closeness and undeniable physical attraction to each other. Hence, the early getaway.

She sighed. All things considered, maybe his leaving was for the best. If she and Jake were not around each other, they couldn't fall more deeply in lust or love with each other, and they couldn't fight.

Maggie smiled as Wyatt and Rusty bounded into the breakfast room. "Hi, guys," she greeted them fondly. "Sleep well?"

They nodded and slipped into their chairs. "Maggie said we're grounded today, so no TV," Wyatt announced solemnly to Harry.

Harry lifted a brow and looked first at the boys, then at Maggie. "Is that so?" Harry drawled.

Maggie nodded. "They made a big mess with their shampoo during their showers last night." So had she and Jake. "It took Jake and me quite a while to clean it up." Too long.

"So what are we gonna do today if we can't watch TV or play outside?" Rusty asked.

Good question. She wished she had known it was going to be raining when she had decided what privilege they would lose today, in penance for their misbehavior.

"Well, there are always your toys," Maggie said.

Unfortunately, the toys lost their amusement value well before noon. Maggie read stories to them for an hour, and colored with them for yet another hour. And still it continued to rain. "When's it gonna stop raining?" Wyatt asked restlessly, staring out the window, chin in hand.

"Not until tomorrow or the next day," Maggie told them after checking the weather on the radio in the kitchen. "There's a hurricane stalled off the coast of Texas, and it's sending huge storms our way."

Rusty groaned. "I'm gonna go crazy, cooped up inside," he lamented emotionally.

Maggie knew the feeling well, and it was only 2:00 p.m. She was going to have to think of something really interesting to do, if she wanted the time to fly by, until Jake returned.

"REALLY? We're going to play Texas settlers?" Rusty asked as Maggie opened the door leading to the usually off-limits third floor.

"Cool!" Wyatt decreed, as Maggie led the way up the stairs.

"How do we do it?" Rusty demanded, raising his voice slightly to be heard over the rain drumming on the rooftop overhead.

The old-fashioned way, by using lots of imagination, Maggie thought. "Well, first we look for some Old West clothes to wear," she told the twins enthusiastically. "Harry said he thought there might be some old bandannas and chaps or vests and hats and stuff up here."

"So we can dress up?" Wyatt asked, looking pretty excited about that.

"Yep. If I can find the stuff," Maggie said.

She switched on the overhead lights as they reached the third floor and was delighted with what she found.

The spacious attic ran the entire length of the sprawling ranch house. Maggie guessed it encompassed a good square twenty-five hundred to three thousand feet. Dormer windows on either end of the attic let in the misty gray daylight, while rain continued to drum against the roof with soothing regularity.

Together, she and the boys surveyed the wealth of belongings scattered across the wood floor. Old-fashioned rocking chairs fought for space between heavy leather-bound steamer trunks. There were several old saddles, kept, Maggie guessed, for sentimental value, and to her amazement, an old teepee, covered with a thin coating of dust.

"Cool," Rusty said, immediately heading for the teepee. "Can we sit inside this, Maggie?"

"Yeah, Unka Jake let us sit in it the last time we were here and it rained real hard. He let us watch while he put it together, too. The teepee used to be his, you know, when he was a kid."

Maggie peered in. Inside, was a stack of very old comic books, a flashlight, and a rolled-out sleeping bag. Somehow she could imagine a much younger Jake playing in here and wanting his nephews to do the same.

Deciding the teepee seemed sturdy enough, Maggie said, "Sure. You can sit on the sleeping bag and pretend you're Indians having a powwow while I look for those old cowboy vests."

The boys scrambled inside while Maggie viewed the crammed attic. Where would those clothes be? she wondered. Harry had mentioned something about a trunk. But there were at least fifteen or more trunks up here. Sighing, she threaded her way through the belongings and headed for the trunk clear at the other end of the attic, next to the settee. She would start with that one, and work her way back, methodically looking through each one.

While the boys played, she sat on the settee and opened the trunk, and was stunned by what she saw. For in it was a photo of a very young Jake, in a tuxedo, his arm around a very young and beautiful bride. Beneath that was what appeared to be a white satin wedding dress and veil, carefully wrapped in tissue paper. And beneath that were other things as well....

"Hey, Maggie!" Wyatt and Rusty poked their heads out of the front of the teepee. "Find any chaps for us yet?"

Feeling abruptly guilty, as though she had been deliberately spying on Jake "marriage-is-not-for-me" MacIntyre, Maggie quickly shut the lid. "Not yet," she called back cheerfully. But she had found something that might explain a lot about Jake and his current hands-off attitude about marriage.

Sabrina'd said the cowboy of Maggie's dreams had a broken heart, in need of mending.... Here, at last, was proof of that.

She would explore it later, when the boys weren't around.

Standing, Maggie dusted her pants off and headed over to the next trunk. In it, were linens and dishes. The next trunk held decorations for the Christmas tree. In the fourth, she hit pay dirt. "Guys," Maggie said, holding up an old Western shirt and battered leather vest that had definitely seen better days. "I think we found exactly what we need."

"I NEVER WOULD'VE figured dressing up like cowpokes on the trail would have entertained those boys for six hours straight," Harry told Maggie, once the boys were asleep.

Maggie smiled, and gave Harry a hand with the last of the dishes. "You helped a lot, by pretending to be a real chuck wagon cook and giving us a bonafide out-on-the-range dinner of chicken-fried steak and taters, sourdough biscuits, green beans and wild blackberry pie."

Harry grinned. "I never saw those little dickens eat so much at one sitting," he confessed happily.

"It was delicious. But then, everything you cook, Harry, is always delicious." Jake was lucky to have Harry around.

"Thanks." Harry grinned at Maggie. "Though personally, I think it was probably the tin plates and mugs that were the real attraction."

Maggie had to agree the camping equipment had added a certain allure. "That, and eating our dinner on the family room floor, in front of the fireplace," she commented. Finished drying the campfire dishes, Maggie stacked them neatly. "Any word from Jake?"

"No, but he said this morning not to expect him back until very late, so I expect it'll be after midnight before he rolls in, knowing Jake."

Maggie nodded. She wondered if Jake was out satisfying his need for hot wild passionate affairs with someone else, then pushed the unexpectedly jealous thought away. Whether Jake was or not, was none of her business. She had no claim on him, after all. Just as he had no claim on her, and the way things were going, never would have, either.

Aware Harry was watching her, Maggie forced a smile. "I think I'll take these campfire dishes up to the attic and tidy up a bit before I go to bed."

"Want some help?" Harry asked.

"No." Maggie shook her head. What she really wanted and needed was to be alone, for just a little while. "I can handle it, thanks."

Once in the attic, Maggie went straight to the trunk where she'd gotten the camp dishes, and put them neatly inside. From there, she replaced the vests, shirts and hats.

Unable to help herself, she looked at the trunk next to the settee. The curiosity she felt was overwhelming.

Transfixed, Maggie stared at the trunk. If Jake had been married before, and she guessed he had, why hadn't he told her so? Had he been through a bad divorce? Was that why he was so turned off about marriage? Had his wife run away from him, or maybe cheated on him by having a hot passionate affair herself?

The clues were in that trunk. All she had to do was go and have another look. And no one would ever be the wiser.

Maggie sighed as she headed for the trunk. She shouldn't be doing this, she told herself guiltily. And yet, by the same token, she couldn't stay away. Darn it all, she wanted to marry a cowboy and the cowboy she wanted to marry was Jake and she would never accomplish that unless she found the key to unlock his heart. The key was in that trunk; she was sure of it.

Chin set determinedly, Maggie knelt before the trunk and lifted the latch.

AN HOUR LATER, Jake shook the water from his long black duster, removed his Stetson and stepped inside the Rollicking M ranch house. Harry, clad in robe and pajamas, had been switching off the lights downstairs and was on his way to bed. "Glad to see you made it back," Harry said warmly. "It's still coming down like gangbusters out there."

Jake hung his coat and hat on the tall rack beside the door. "You're telling me. The drive home from Houston was miserable." Made more so by the fact he couldn't get Maggie off his mind. This, despite her irritating decision to continue her great husband hunt.

"Did you get something to eat?" Harry asked, concerned. "If not, I could warm you up some dinner."

"I'm fine, Harry. Got a bit to eat before I left the city. Thanks, anyway." Jake paused to hang his coat on the rack to dry. Though only 10:00 p.m., it was awfully quiet. He glanced around, scanning for any sign of trouble, finding none. "How are Maggie and the boys?"

"They're doing great," Harry confided. "Weather being what it was, they had to work to keep themselves entertained, though."

*I'll bet they did.* In a way, Jake was sorry he missed it. Playing inside on a rainy day sounded like fun.

"So how'd Maggie manage?" Jake asked.

Harry smiled, revealing without meaning to how fond he had become of their guest and temporary nanny in only four days. "She went up in the attic and rooted around 'til she found some dress-up clothes for the kids, and then they played Western settlers the rest of the day."

Briefly, Harry went on to explain about cowpoke

costumes and makeshift wagon trails, but all Jake could think about was the attic, and the fact Maggie had been up there, looking around. Searching. For God only knew what…besides the costumes.

He swallowed around the sudden tightening of his throat. Damn it, he thought furiously, if she'd found any of that stuff he'd hidden away, even inadvertently…

"Jake? You okay?" Harry asked, undisguised apprehension on his face. He stepped nearer. "You're looking kind of pale, all of a sudden."

"I'm just tired." Jake shrugged it off and regarded Harry with a respect and affection that had been years in the making. "Go on to bed, Harry. And don't worry about the rest of the lights. I'll close up down here."

And then, Jake told himself grimly, he was going to go up to the attic and find out just what—if anything—Maggie Porter had unearthed.

"WHAT IN BLAZES do you think you're doing?" Jake's voice, low and lethally angry, came out of the darkness from the other end of the attic, startling Maggie into dropping the tiny pink-and-white baby clothes in her hands.

Before she could do much more than replace them in the trunk, beneath the pictures, wedding gown and veil, Jake stormed the length of the room, his boots echoing on the unvarnished wood floor, and yanked her to her feet. Dressed in Levi jeans, an open-collared blue cotton shirt and a Harris tweed blazer, the hint of evening beard and lingering traces of his cologne clinging to his jaw, he had never looked sexier. Nor more out of sorts.

"I expect you feel I owe you an apology," Maggie said, willing herself to hold her own with him. Though it might have been easier had she arranged her hair in something other than a high, bouncy ponytail atop her head, or been clad in something more dignified than white sneakers, denim walking shorts, a white T-shirt and blue work shirt.

"I expect an apology and then some," Jake affirmed grimly, accusation flashing in his dark eyes.

Maggie stiffened but couldn't quite bring herself to shrug off his grip. "I didn't come up here looking for this."

"But you found it anyway." His voice was unforgiving.

"Yes, I did, while searching for cowpoke clothes for the twins. Damn it, Jake, why didn't you tell me you were married before?" Maggie asked, abruptly losing her balance and stumbling backward as he finally let her go.

"Because it was none of your business," he said gruffly, looking as if he expected her to argue with him about that, too.

"What happened, Jake?" she asked quietly, in an attempt to assure him that it was all right, even advisable, to confide in her. She wanted desperately to get to the heartache that had so negatively impacted his life. "Why are there baby clothes in this trunk?" She started to tuck a strand of hair behind her ear, but when she realized her fingers were trembling, she abruptly stopped. "Is the reason you're so dead set against having a wife and children because you've already had a wife and child?" If so, it made sense.

Jake swallowed, and to her frustration, looked all

the more remote. "I'm not getting into this with you, Maggie."

The hell he wasn't. "What happened to your wife, Jake?" Maggie persisted boldly.

Jake blew out an exasperated breath. "She died, okay?"

And it had obviously hurt him like hell. Maggie bore that knowledge like a lethal blow to her chest. She forced herself to draw a breath and look into his dark brooding eyes. "And your baby?" she whispered, afraid from the devastated look on his face, she already knew the answer to that, too. "What happened to your baby, Jake?"

Pain drew the skin taut across his face. His cheekbones stood out in sharp relief. Looking, for one long heartbreaking moment as though he would've done anything to change the outcome, he announced simply, angrily, "The baby died, too."

MAGGIE GASPED softly, in a combination of horror at what he'd been through, and shared pain. She had imagined a bitter, ugly divorce. Or a runaway wife who'd taken his baby with her, too. But not this. Never this. And then she knew. The cowboy that Sabrina'd seen in her crystal ball, the cowboy who had been lingering outside the fence that surrounded two graves, had been Jake.

Sabrina had told her that he'd have to mend his broken heart before he could love again. It was up to Maggie to help him do that. She had never wanted anything more than to help him recover.

"Oh, Jake—" she said softly, her heart going out to him all over again, for all he had suffered, and was not yet over. She was beginning to understand at long last why he worked so hard to keep others at bay.

"Are you satisfied now?" he retorted angrily. Looking more hurt and upset than she had ever seen him, he shouldered rudely past her.

Maggie grabbed his arm, knowing the hardest things to face were also the most critical, knowing it was imperative he do so now, before any more time elapsed. He looked down at her hand, where it curved around his biceps, and she knew he was silently debating whether or not to jerk his arm away. She glanced up into his eyes and saw the resentment.

Slowly, she released her hold on him. Stepped back. But did not—would not—give up. "Are the deaths of your wife and child the reason you don't want to marry again?"

Jake stiffened involuntarily, his broad shoulders straining against the Harris tweed blazer and blue cotton shirt. "I had it all once, and that is more than most people ever get."

"So," Maggie retorted, a little angrily, "you're not willing to risk anything?" *Not even for us and what we might have if you'd only let us?*

"Not in my personal life, no, I'm not," Jake growled, looking even more provoked.

Again he started past her, and again Maggie blocked his path. She planted both hands on her hips, and told him sternly, "You're a fool if you never allow yourself to love, Jake."

He looked down at her, his sensual lips curving into a cynical, warning smile. "And you, Maggie, are playing with fire."

Ignoring the shivers of reaction ghosting down her

spine, she spread her palms wide in a beseeching gesture. "Don't you see you have to let go of your grief?"

Jake's jaw tightened. He looked past her, toward the other end of the darkened attic. His expression was thunderous again. "Back off, Maggie."

Easier said than done, she thought defiantly. "I can't back off, not when I see you hurting as much as you obviously are." She paused, searching with all her heart for a way to get through to him, to bring him out of the heartache-filled past and into the possibility-filled future. "Don't you understand, Jake?" she continued softly, persuasively. "I have to comfort you. I want to comfort you."

Jake slanted her a dark, assessing glance. "The only kind of comfort I want is this," he said, hauling her against him. Before Maggie could do much more than gasp her astonishment, his mouth fused with hers, his tongue hungrily forced her lips open. Angry at the way he was treating her, at the way he was using sex to drive them apart, instead of bring them together, she flattened her palms against his shoulders and shoved with all her might.

Which was, she decided in chagrin mere seconds later, exactly what he had wanted her to do all along.

"You see, Maggie?" Jake said roughly, dropping his hands, victoriously stepping back. "I'm not what you want. I'm not what you need."

Nor, Maggie thought, deeply disappointed and even more hurt, did he want to be.

"Now get out of here," Jake continued gruffly, refusing to meet her eyes and turning away.

Once again, Maggie calculated the odds and squared

off with him like a boxer entering the ring. "Like hell I will," she retorted. "You listen to me, Jake Mac-Intyre, and you listen good." She grabbed his shirt-front, crumpling the starched fabric in her fist, and forced him to face her. "If anyone is going to be the judge of what I need, it's going to be me."

# Chapter Ten

Jake looked down at the grip she had on his shirt, then stuck his hands in his pockets and regarded her with an unsmiling expression. "You are one stubborn woman," he accused softly.

Her hands tightening on his shirt, Maggie defiantly held his gaze and stood her ground. "You haven't seen anything yet."

Which was, Jake thought, exactly what he was afraid of. Knowing he had to prove himself a real bastard to get rid of her, and he had to get rid of her lest he break her heart, Jake took both her hands in his and wordlessly released her grip on his shirt. Aware she was watching him, spellbound, he sauntered over to another trunk, yanked up the lid and hauled out an armful of blankets. He tossed them onto the floor. Then reached into the pocket of his jeans and pulled out several condoms he'd bought earlier that evening, while assuring himself all the while he was not going to need them.

"If you stay—" he said gruffly, tossing the condoms down onto the blankets, holding her eyes with his as he matter-of-factly unfastened his belt "—I'm going to make love to you right here and right now.'' To further demonstrate his intentions, he unknotted the blue work shirt she had tied at her waist. ''And it is not,'' he warned softly and seriously, ''going to be the romantic interlude of your dreams.''

But Maggie, rather than be offended by his unchivalrous attitude, merely tossed down the blue work shirt, kicked off her tennis shoes and released her hair from the high bouncy ponytail. Thusly prepared, and clad in shorts and a white T-shirt, she held her arms aloft and offered herself for the taking. ''Then get to it, cowboy,'' she drawled, surprising him all the more as she gave him a sexy, determined look that spoke volumes about her intent. '''Cause I think we've wasted far too much time finding each other to delay even one second longer.''

Despite the condoms and the blankets, the way he'd already started to undress them, she didn't think he'd do it—he could see it in her face. Well, this was one cowboy who was going to prove her wrong time and time again, Jake thought resolutely, as he swept her into his arms and lowered her onto the pile of quilts. He followed her down, stretching out overtop her.

Expecting her to protest at his brusque matter-of-fact approach to lovemaking, he was stunned when she instead took his face in her hands and swiftly, purposefully lowered his head to hers.

He knew he shouldn't do it, knew he shouldn't anchor her to him this way—even for one night—but he no longer gave a damn. He slanted his lips over hers and tipping her head up to allow him greater access, he gave in to the incessant ache to be close to her and bestowed upon her the intimate kiss she desired.

As her lips molded to his, and her tongue sensually twined with his, he kissed her harshly, then desperately, then sweetly, until he felt the need pouring out of her, mingling with the desire and the temper and the even fiercer need to comfort him. And beneath that, he felt the tenderness that was as much a bewitching and elemental part of her as it was unexpected.

He knew he hadn't done anything to deserve Maggie's love. Nor had he ever expected a woman—any woman—to be able to make him want again. Maggie did. He hadn't expected a woman to lure him into taking a risk. Yet here he was, entangled with Maggie on the blankets in the attic...positioned between her legs...kissing her long and hard and deep, and running his fingers through her soft blond hair. And still knowing, even as he kissed her with a slow, insistent demand, and felt her melt helplessly beneath him, that it wasn't nearly enough...and wouldn't be, until he had made her his and his alone.

When his hand slipped beneath the T-shirt, and cupped her breast through the thin lace of her bra, she trembled with pleasure. He moved his hips against hers insistently, in the same rhythm as his tongue in her mouth, and she moaned on a soft, shuddering breath, her nipple beading against his palm.

His body trembling with the effort it was costing him to go slow enough to please her, he pulled her fractionally closer, wanting her to the point of madness, yet knowing she deserved so much more than anything he had given her thus far. He might not be able to give her what she wanted or needed in a man or potential husband, but he could give her this night.

He could make love to her in a way neither of them would ever forget....

Maggie hadn't expected Jake to come back in time to find her in the attic, but considering the way the events had transpired, she thought as he deftly divested her of her bra and shorts, she wasn't sorry he had. She had never wanted to be as close to a man as she wanted to be to Jake. And considering the fierce expression of longing on his face, the almost primal possessiveness in the way he undressed her and let her help him undress and put on his condom, he felt the same way. For tonight, she decided as he lay her back on the blankets, parted her thighs with one hot, smooth motion of his palms, and slid between them once again, that would be enough. It would have to be.

"Tell me what you want," he whispered, his dark eyes glittering with anticipation, as he kissed her thoroughly and slid down to worship the blond triangle between her legs.

Maggie arched her back and caught his head in her hands. Her answer was wrenched from her, right along with her shuddering response. "You, Jake. I want you."

"Tell me what you need," he said, his hands rhythmically and thoroughly caressing her ankles, her knees, the delicate insides of her thighs.

"Is it this?"

Her eyes drifted shut and she sighed as his lips found her center.

"Or is it this?" Gently, he tested her readiness with the tip of his finger.

Shimmers of excitement swept through her as the scent of his aftershave and the clean soap scent of his skin combined with his nakedness to tantalize her unbearably. She clasped his shoulders tightly. "I need this, Jake. I need tonight." *I need you, Jake, and only you.*

"Heaven help me, I need tonight, too," he murmured, the emotional tone in his voice nearly undoing her.

Toes pointed, she arched and came apart beneath him in hot, aching waves. With a low grunt of satisfaction, he moved higher. His manhood brushed against her thighs, setting off another lightning storm of reaction.

"I didn't realize how much," he continued his confession raggedly as he surged inside her.

The heat of their joining seared and enveloped her in a pleasure unlike anything Maggie had ever known. Like a whirlwind, the fierceness of their lovemaking swept them both into its power. They clung together, moving in unison, moving toward the peak. She let him lift her higher and raise her knees. She let him possess her fiercely, almost desperately, singlemindedly catapulting her to new heights, and when it was over, she did not let go, but rather, enticed him into making love again, more slowly this time, with the tenderness, depth of sensuality, and slow mutuality of purpose they both deserved.

Afterward, as they cuddled against each other, the rain still beating softly and steadily overhead, she could feel how much he needed and wanted her, even if it would be light-years before he would ever admit it. And that made all the difference in the world. If it were up to her, Maggie thought, holding him all the tighter as the love poured out of her, Jake would never be alone or lonely again.

It was time to rip up her list and start planning that engagement announcement for the Houston newspaper. She'd found the man for her. The only man for her.

"HEY, UNKA JAKE, how come Maggie's calling you Wounded Bear today?" Rusty demanded as he and his twin brother tore into Jake's den.

*'Cause I've been acting like a complete jerk,* Jake thought, *and I don't even know why.* He just knew he had been sad and out of sorts ever since he and Maggie had made love the night before. "I'm just tired, Rusty," Jake explained. "And when I'm tired I get grumpy. That's why I came in here and shut the door. So I wouldn't be grumpy around anyone else."

"Well, it's too late," Wyatt added, bursting in to join the conversation, "'cause Maggie jus' told Harry that if you get any grumpier someone's gonna have to take you out and shoot you."

At that, Jake found himself grinning despite his foul mood. He punched in a Save instruction on his computer, so he wouldn't lose any of the data he had just typed. Turning toward the twins, he leaned back in his desk chair and, unable to help himself, asked, "Where is Maggie, anyway?"

Wyatt pushed around the desk and climbed up on one side of Jake's lap; Rusty climbed up on the other. "She's in the kitchen, on the telephone, talkin' to her New York agent."

A warning sounded in Jake's head. And though he

knew it was wrong to nose around in anyone else's business, he asked anyway, "What about?"

"Oh, he wants her to come back to work right away and Maggie keeps laughing like this—" Wyatt did an imitation of a flirty female laugh "—and telling him no, she's not coming back for even that much money, that if he wants her back he's going to have to do better than that even!"

Wants her back, Jake thought, alarmed.

As client, or girlfriend?

Was it possible Maggie was in Texas only because she was running from some painful romantic past, too?

He didn't like the thought. Frowning, he pushed away the image of Maggie with another man and stood. It was past time he took a break. "You know, guys, I think I could use a glass of lemonade. How about you?"

MAGGIE WAS STILL laughing softly when Jake entered the kitchen. The receiver pressed to her ear, she had her back to him. And even though he reminded himself coldly that she had every right to flirt with whomever she damn well pleased, his gut tightened at the thought she might be involved with someone else who didn't particularly want to get married, or have children, either.

"All right. I'll call you if I change my mind. I promise. But I wouldn't count on it," Maggie spoke into the phone. Smiling, she hung up.

"Wounded Bear wants some lemonade!" Rusty announced.

Maggie, who—rather than interact with Jake—had already resumed assisting Harry make a batch of chocolate chip cookies, had the grace to flush at Rusty's comment. Which perversely only made Jake want to embarrass her all the more. "Wounded Bear?" Jake echoed, sardonically lifting his brow.

The pink in Maggie's cheeks deepened prettily as she turned away from him and slid a cookie sheet into the oven. "I assure you I don't know what they are talking about," she said stiffly.

"Sure you do, Maggie." Rusty paused to sneak a bit of cookie batter from the spoon. "After all, you been callin' Unka Jake Wounded Bear all day."

Thus exposed, Maggie gave up the ruse. Still avoiding Jake's eyes, she shrugged indifferently at his nephews. "It seemed appropriate."

Jake knew it. He wasn't proud of it. He was acting like a donkey's rear end. They were going to have to talk sometime, but when?

Before he could figure that out, the phone rang. "I'll get it!" Wyatt said. He grabbed the receiver, lifted it clumsily to his ear, and said, "Rollicking M Ranch, Wyatt speaking. Mama! Hi!" Wyatt listened a moment, a wide grin spreading across his face. "Hurrah, hurrah! Okay." Wyatt handed the phone to Jake. "Mama wants to talk to you, Unka Jake."

Aware Maggie was watching him carefully as she lifted cooled cookies off another baking sheet onto a plate, Jake picked up the phone. "Hi, sis, what's up?" As he listened, Jake smiled, too. "That's great, Kelsey. Yeah, anytime is fine with me." Jake handed the phone to Rusty. "Your mama wants to talk to you a minute."

"Good news?" Harry asked Jake, as he spooned batter onto yet another cookie pan.

"The best," Jake confirmed, trying not to look at Maggie. "Kelsey found Clint and he's agreed to try to work things out. The two of them should be back in Texas in a few days to pick up the boys."

"That's great," Maggie interjected, as abruptly aware as Jake that her reason for staying at the ranch was coming to an end. Her face unusually pale, she turned away from Jake and Harry, wiped her hands on a dish towel and removed her apron. "Listen, if you men will excuse me for a minute," she said in a muffled voice, keeping her back to all four guys, "I just remembered something I have to do."

"YOU'RE UPSET, aren't you?" Jake said, following Maggie out into the rainswept flower gardens, on the other side of the pool.

"Why would I be upset?" Maggie said, trying hard to retain her composure in the face of so much emotional turmoil. She had known this was coming. Why should she feel so surprised? Never mind so disappointed. Like the best thing that had ever happened to her was being taken away before she had the chance to enjoy it. She knelt to snip a fragrant yellow rose. "I want Wyatt and Rusty to be reunited with their folks."

Jake hunkered down beside her. He held the bush, so the thorny stems wouldn't catch on her gardening glove. "Do you also want to leave?"

Maggie slipped the cut flower into her basket and sat back on her heels. If it was all-out honesty he wanted, all-out honesty was what he was going to get. "Considering the way you've been acting today, it might be a good thing." She'd known all along that the boys were the only reason he had ever invited her into his life, even for a little while, because he needed her help taking care of them. Still, after the passionate way they had made love in the attic, she would've thought he would be happy today. Instead, he was moping around, looking and acting as if he'd lost his best friend, and behaving toward her as if nothing the least bit special had happened anyway. Both attitudes rankled.

Deciding she'd had enough of his company, Maggie surged to her feet. Jake vaulted up after her and then invaded her space until they were standing toe-to-toe. "Look, I tried to be straight with you," he said, as if that excused everything.

Maggie tossed her head. "Straight or just cold to the bone?" she retorted, able to tell immediately by the look on his face that she'd hit a nerve.

His jaw tightened obstinately. He braced his hands loosely on his waist, then towered over her, his voice dropping another intimate notch. "I don't deny that last night we may have tumbled into something neither of us was really ready for."

Maggie laughed bitterly. How like him to excuse his behavior as something beyond his control, when he'd known exactly what he was doing last night and so had she.

"Speak for yourself, Jake," she ordered tightly, moving on to the next rosebush.

Still dogging her every step, he watched her add several white roses to her basket. "What's that supposed to mean?"

Maggie sighed. As long as she was in for a penny, she might as well be in for a pound. She straightened reluctantly, swiveled to face him. "If you want my opinion—"

"I asked, didn't I?" Jake interrupted bearishly.

Maggie's glance narrowed warningly at his tone. "I think you're just plain scared of allowing yourself to love again," she said, and when he didn't respond, she stepped nearer and tried again. "If you want my opinion, I think you're still so busy being faithful to your wife that you have no time for any woman in the present, including me."

She expected him to be upset by her assertion; to her astonishment, he wasn't, not at all. "I don't deny I will always feel married to my wife in my heart," Jake said matter-of-factly. At the hurt on her face, he paused. "Look, I didn't lie to you when I said I wasn't the marrying kind. I was married once. Happily. I'm not getting married again."

"So you've said." She started to step past.

He curved a delaying hand on her shoulder. "Let me finish," he said gruffly, searching her upturned face before he continued. "But I do believe in hot affairs, passion and fleeting happiness. That we could have, Maggie, in abundance, for as long as you want it," he said softly, increasing his hold on her ever so slightly, before letting go of her altogether, stepping back. "But that's all we could have."

Bitterness rose in Maggie's throat. "How generous of you."

"Hey, you knew what you were getting into last night when you slept with me and you let yourself make love with me anyway."

Yes, Maggie thought, she had. Because that was

what it had been to her, making love. But that didn't mean she had to further her mistake.

"What are you thinking?" Jake asked.

Maggie sighed and shook her head. "That if I was smart, I'd kick you out of my life as far and fast as possible. And resurrect my wish list, pronto." And this time, Maggie vowed sternly, she'd look for a man who not only loved kids but could control them, a man who actually wanted to marry, who did not put business above all.

"What else?" Jake asked.

*That I love you,* she thought, *desperately.*

Otherwise, she never would have given herself to him.

"Maggie?"

"I know you want me to give up on the idea of us," she admitted finally.

He nodded, his expression relieved. "In any permanent sense, yes, I do."

Maggie tilted her head up to his. "But I can't, Jake." She bit her lip. "Maybe I'm a fool, but I just can't."

The sound of running footsteps sounded on the patio. It was followed by the sound of a throat clearing. Maggie and Jake turned in unison to see Harry and the twins grinning at them.

"The boys and I would like to see a movie and have dinner out, if it is all right with the two of you," Harry said.

"Yeah, Harry thinks it'll help Unka Jake stop being so cranky if he spends time with you, Maggie," Rusty reported gleefully, causing Wyatt to giggle madly.

"Shh!" Harry admonished them both, while Jake

and Maggie both flushed with embarrassment. "Well?" Harry asked, patiently awaiting their decision.

There was no time like the present to lasso that cowboy she had always wanted. "Sounds great, Harry," Maggie said impulsively, giving her stamp of approval to the plan. "Thank you."

Beside her, Jake hesitated visibly. At his lack of enthusiasm the boys' faces fell. Evidently, goaded by conscience, Jake relented and gave in with forced cheerfulness. "That sounds good, Harry," he said. "We'll grab something here."

"Oh, that won't be necessary," Harry interrupted, giving Jake a look that reminded Jake to be a gentleman. "Maggie has already arranged for you two to have dinner out."

"I made reservations at Brenner's in Houston. My treat," Maggie said quickly, lest he think she was out to take advantage of him in any way, including monetarily. "Harry told me they've got the best steaks in Houston, if not the world." She forced a smile. "So I thought we'd try it."

"C'mon boys, let's go get cleaned up while Maggie and Jake work out the details of their evening together," Harry said.

Jake waited until Harry and the boys had departed. As soon as he and Maggie were alone again, his mask of politeness dropped. "You think you've got everything figured out, don't you?" he said. He looked angry, Maggie noted nervously. Maybe this plan she and Harry had cooked up while baking cookies together was not so foolproof after all. She shifted the basket of cut flowers from one arm to the other. "I—we—

just thought—maybe a change of pace?" she stammered finally.

"And a chance to get me alone might work miracles," Jake guessed grimly.

That, too, Maggie thought. And why not, it had before, she reminded herself, her confidence returning. Darn it all, she knew she could get Jake to stop living out the heartache of his past on a daily basis if she kept working at it. And once he had allowed himself to get over the past, perhaps he'd begin thinking about his future. Their future.

"A little sweet talk never hurt," Maggie said with a shrug. "Our dinner reservations are at eight, by the way."

Jake studied her momentarily, his expression impassive, then glanced at his watch. "Looks like I've got just enough time to take care of things, too, then," he murmured mysteriously and walked off.

Time, Maggie thought, stunned. Time to take care of what?

## Chapter Eleven

"Great, Kirk is already here," Jake noted, as they waited for the friendly wait-staff to seat them in the woodsy dining room at Brenner's. He lifted a hand in a friendly wave to a handsome man across the room. Blond, blue-eyed and athletic in looks, Kirk looked to be in his midthirties. He was dressed in jeans, boots, a Western shirt and suede vest. He had a confident, successful air about him that might have intrigued Maggie, at least on a surface level, had she not already been head over heels in love with Jake.

"I thought we were going to be dining alone," Maggie murmured, surprised and hurt.

Jake chuckled jauntily. "Wrong again, huh, Maggie?"

She turned to face Jake, a smile frozen on her face, her stomach clenching with a mixture of apprehension and disappointment. She couldn't believe he was doing this to her, after she had arranged for them to have some rare time alone, away from Harry and the boys, and their first real evening out together. If he had meant to hurt her, he had.

"Don't look so glum," Jake said, clamping a reassuring hand on her slender shoulder. He leaned down to whisper in her ear. "Kirk Sutherland should be the perfect man for you. He's a true cowboy, who owns his own ranch and even rides rodeo on the weekends when he has time. He also meets every qualification on that wish list you are always talking about."

Maggie looked into Jake's eyes. She searched his face for any sign of remorse but saw none. Whatever closeness they had shared seemed to be gone. With a stab of disappointment she realized all his emotional barriers were up. He was still married to his late wife, at least in his heart. She realized sadly that might not ever change. If it didn't, there was no hope for the two of them.

Hand pressed lightly to her spine, Jake steered her toward the table where Kirk Sutherland was seated. Briefly, he made introductions and held out Maggie's chair for her.

Hoping the evening would somehow get better, if she just acted as if nothing were wrong, too, Maggie slid into the chair Jake held out for her, only to have Jake step away. He gave them both a brief, officious smile that acted like a splash of cold water on Maggie's already ravaged nerves. "I'll see you-all later, then," he said. Without a backward glance, he sauntered out of the restaurant.

"I can't believe it." Kirk beamed at Maggie the second they were alone. He poured Maggie a glass of Lone Star beer and continued, still shaking his handsome blond head in awe, "When Jake told me he'd gotten me a blind date with *the* Maggie Porter of *Sports Illustrated* fame, I thought he was pulling my leg." Kirk sighed happily. "Guess not."

Maggie forced a smile as she took the glass Kirk handed her. There was no use encouraging Kirk, because he hadn't a chance in the world with her. "Did he also tell you that I want to marry a rich man?" she asked her date calmly, for once hoping Jake had made her sound as cold-blooded and opportunistic as possible, because if that didn't turn off Kirk, she thought with a beleaguered inner sigh, nothing would.

"Actually, he mentioned it," Kirk replied matter-of-factly, looking not the least bit put off by the revelation. "But that's okay with me. 'Cause I've always wanted to marry an exceptionally beautiful woman and you are that, Maggie Porter."

She narrowed her glance at Kirk, wondering if he was as much a victim of Jake's not-so-nice matchmaking as she was. And if that was the case, as she guessed it was, given his attitude, what other laudable qualities did the easygoing Kirk have?

"Then you are wealthy?" she asked. Amazing as it seemed, this potential husband Jake had picked out for her really did seem to be on the level.

"Yes I am very wealthy as it happens." Kirk grinned happily, clinking the rim of his glass against the rim of hers in a silent toast. "Now, what say you and I order some dinner and get better acquainted..."

"I DARE SAY Maggie can let herself in when she returns from her date," Harry remarked conversationally, shortly after 1:00 a.m. "There's really no reason for you to wait up for her, Jake."

The hell there wasn't, Jake scowled, his mouth thinning into a belligerent line. If things had gone as poorly as usual, Maggie would have been home hours before now.

Damn it all, why hadn't things gone as poorly as usual? No matter how right Kirk looked statistically or otherwise, Jake knew Kirk was no more right for Maggie than any of the other potential husbands he had set her up with.

Aware Harry was still watching him with a faintly judgmental attitude, Jake motioned to the portfolio of stock information on his lap. "I'm not waiting up for Maggie," he said defensively. "I'm trying to make a decision on how much to invest in these technology stocks."

"Right." Harry sent Jake a disbelieving look and stifled a yawn. "Well, give Maggie my regards when she does get in, if she does get in. Meantime, I'm going to bed. Rusty and Wyatt will be up early, expecting breakfast."

"Sleep well," Jake said distractedly.

He waited until Harry had exited the living room then surged to his feet and stalked to the front windows. Damn it all, where was she? he thought irritably, searching the dark Texas night and long ranch house driveway for any signs of her return. Her date should not have taken this long. None of the others had.

But Maggie wasn't home at one in the morning. Or two, or three. By 4:00 a.m., Jake was half out of his mind with worry, imagining her dead on the side of the road somewhere, the victim of an auto accident, or carjacking or God only knew what. And that was when he heard the low purr of Kirk's Cadillac in the drive.

His heart thudding heavily in his chest, Jake surged to the window once again.

The sound of Maggie's soft low laughter and even sexier, softer voice made his gut tighten with jealousy. Jake looked past the edge of the drape. Kirk had an arm draped casually across her shoulders, his Stetson tipped back on his head. He was laughing softly, too, as he sauntered up the sidewalk. Kirk and Maggie paused, ten feet or so from the front door, their bodies illuminated in the soft glow of the porch light.

To Jake's irritation, he could not make out any of what was being said as they whispered to one another with delighted expressions on their faces. But there was no way he could have missed the light, affectionate kiss Kirk pressed to Maggie's brow, or the warm hug he gave her in parting.

"I'll call you then," he promised Maggie audibly, before heading down the walk, toward his car.

Maggie smiled and waved. "I'll look forward to it," she said, waving back. Still smiling, she headed for the front porch. His every muscle tensing, Jake stepped away from the window, just as she walked in.

"Spying on me?" Maggie asked casually, dropping her key into her purse.

Caught in the act, so to speak, Jake saw no reason to deny it. He shrugged and stuck his hands in the pockets of his jeans. "I was curious as to how the date went, since I fixed it up."

Maggie flashed him one of her dazzling cover girl smiles. "Actually, it was great," she replied with a soft contentment that rankled him even more than her air of happiness. Her eyes lasered on his with a look of determination he might have admired under other circumstances. "Kirk is a wonderful guy. I had a very nice time."

The knot in Jake's gut that had been there ever since he'd left her with Kirk, twisted painfully. "Then you're going to see him again?" Jake asked casually, telling himself it meant nothing at all to him if she did.

"Yes, as a matter of fact, I am." Maggie brushed past, her head tipped up regally.

It was all Jake could do not to catch her arm and bring her back to his side. Instead, he turned, his hands still in his pockets, and said, even more casually, "Then you're serious about him?"

Maggie stopped dead in her tracks. She pivoted slowly to face him with a runway model's grace and her own inherent style. Though she'd been out most of the night, to his dismay, she still looked as lovely as she had when he'd left her. Her short black cocktail dress, with its cap sleeves and swirly skirt, bore nary a wrinkle. Her golden hair curled gently about her shoulders, looking as soft and lustrous as the single strand of pearls around her neck.

"Why?" Her chin took on that stubborn tilt he knew so well.

Jake drew a breath and tried not to let on how restless and edgy he felt. "That's not an answer," he replied quietly.

Her pink lips curved in a taunting half smile. Her fair brows lifted. "So?"

"I think I have a right—" he began angrily.

"You have no rights, Jake," Maggie interrupted, an answering fury flashing in her vivid blue eyes. "Not where I'm concerned."

"I think I have every right," Jake countered smoothly, stepping close to inhale the faint, floral fragrance of her perfume. "After all, I set the date up." *Even though it damn near killed me to do so.*

Maggie scoffed and moved past him, through the hallway, toward the kitchen. "You also did it without my knowledge or permission."

Jake defended himself just as hotly, as he followed her close on her heels. "You wanted me to fix you up in exchange for taking care of the boys. I did so."

"Yes." Maggie opened the refrigerator door, retrieved a carton of orange juice, and slammed it on the counter. She stalked to the cabinet and withdrew a glass. "And for that, I'm grateful, because Kirk is a very nice guy and I had a great time with him tonight."

Jake watched her pour herself a glass of juice and down half of it in one long thirsty gulp. Watching her, something warm and soft turned over inside his chest. "What'd you do after you left the restaurant?" he demanded, wondering how much longer he was going to be able to keep his hands off her. He'd stayed away from her all day, and most of the evening, even fixed her up with another man, yet all he could think about was burying himself in her soft, pliant body.

Hell, it had gotten to the point he couldn't even be in the same room with her without wanting to drag her in his arms and kiss her senseless, and that annoyed the heck out of him. It showed a lack of control, and he was a man who prided himself on his control. Or at least he had until Maggie Porter had waltzed into his life.

Maggie flashed him a belligerent look and finished

the rest of her juice. "Why do you care what Kirk and I did on our date?" she demanded with a look that dared him to answer honestly.

"I just want to make sure he treated you right, is all," he said gruffly.

Blotting the moisture from the edges of her lips with the tips of her fingers, Maggie lifted her eyes to his and announced, with no small measure of irony, "Well, he did."

Jake picked up the glass she set down, filled it with juice. Putting his lips where hers had been, he drank deeply, too. "Did you sleep with him?"

Maggie's lips dropped open in a round O of surprise. For a long moment, she simply stared at him. Finally, she scoffed in derision, shook her head at him, and drawled pointedly, "Cowboy, you are way out of line."

Maybe so. Jake still had to know. "Did you?" he demanded again, even more urgently.

Temper flashed in Maggie's deep blue eyes as she attempted to stalk past. "If you want to know so badly, ask him!"

Jake clamped a hand on her arm and hauled her around to face him. He'd done all this, knowing it would be only a matter of time before she went the way of the others and gave up on the idea of a future with him, too. But she hadn't. And he didn't know how much longer he could stay away from her. Not when she looked so damn beautiful. Not when she looked at him the way she did, like she wanted to personally and immediately heal every ache in his lonesome heart.

"You didn't, did you?"

Again, Maggie scoffed. She edged nearer, so her breasts lightly brushed his chest. "Why do you care, Mr. I-Only-Embark-On-Hot-Passionate-Affairs?" she asked in a soft bedroom voice that only made him want to kiss and hold her all the more.

"Because I don't want to see you hurt," Jake said gruffly, aware that in the short time he'd been talking with her, he'd grown painfully hard.

Maggie stepped even closer, so her thighs brushed his. "Then you shouldn't have made love to me last night."

Jake adjusted his grip on her. "As I recall," he recounted, his voice hard as nails as he let her go at long last and stepped back, putting some physical distance between them, "that was a two-way street."

"You think I don't know that?" Maggie said, tears glimmering in her eyes. With a trembling hand, she picked up the orange juice carton and set it back in the refrigerator. Her back to him, she carried her glass over to the dishwasher and carefully slipped it into the upper dish rack. "I thought— Oh, never mind what I thought!" Hands raised in a gesture of defense, she marched past him.

"What?" Jake demanded. Irritated she hadn't finished, he stepped to bar her exit from the kitchen.

Maggie stopped dead in her tracks. He lounged in the doorway, arms folded loosely in front of him, his right hip and shoulder resting against the frame.

"I thought you were capable of loving someone again," she told him in a voice strangely devoid of emotion for someone so visibly upset. "But obviously you're not, because if you were, you wouldn't have set me up without my knowledge and then dumped me on someone else the way you did tonight. But not to worry, Jake." She pinned him with a look of quiet dignity and adapted a reasonable tone that was somehow all the more alarming, "Your plan to get rid of me ASAP worked." Maggie paused and lifted her chin as if daring him to try to get her to do otherwise. "I'll be leaving as soon as Kelsey and her husband Clint return to collect their boys."

"GOSH, MAGGIE, you look tired," Wyatt said.

"Yeah, what happened, didn't you get much sleep?" Rusty asked, between mouthfuls of hot cereal.

Aware Harry was watching her carefully, and that these days she was wearing her heart on her sleeve all too frequently, Maggie headed straight for the coffeemaker and said, "I had a late night."

"Then you enjoyed your date with Kirk Sutherland?" Harry asked.

Maggie lifted her hand noncommittally, amazed at how much it hurt her to recall such a splendidly pleasant and uneventful evening. "Yes and no." Maggie smiled at Harry warmly, knowing that whatever was going on here, Harry was not to blame. "Kirk's a great guy, no doubt about it. Funny, successful, handsome, interested in marriage and children, just like I am."

"But—?" Harry pressed.

*He's not Jake.* Wary of revealing too much of her feelings, lest they get immediately back to Jake, Maggie merely shrugged helplessly. "There just wasn't any chemistry. I can see Kirk being a friend. A good friend, actually."

"But nothing more," Harry guessed, ladling cereal into a bowl and handing it to Maggie.

"Right." She sat at the table and stirred her oatmeal listlessly.

"Unka Jake went out riding this morning," Wyatt announced.

"Yeah, he's grumpy, too, 'cause he said he didn't get much sleep, either," Rusty reported.

Finished with their cereal, they pushed their bowls away. "Maggie, if we're not grounded any more can we go watch cartoons on TV in the family room this morning?" Wyatt asked.

"We'll be good so's we won't lose our priv'leges again," Rusty promised.

"I think that would be a very good idea," Maggie said.

The boys carefully carried their dishes to the sink for Harry to wash, then tore out. Harry poured himself a cup of coffee and sat down opposite Maggie. She didn't know quite how it happened, but in the short time she had been at the Rollicking M Ranch Harry had become as much a father figure to her as he had to Jake.

Harry, being Harry, cut right to the chase. "You love Jake, don't you?"

To her horror, Maggie felt her eyes fill with tears. She swallowed hard as she met his eyes. "For all the good it will do me."

Harry patted her arm compassionately. "Give him time."

"If I thought it was just that—" Unable to eat another bite of the hot, delicious cereal, Maggie pushed her bowl away and briefly buried her face in her hands. "I would wait for him, Harry," she confessed in a muffled voice laced with regret. "I'd wait as long as it took. But I don't think he is ever going to stop feeling married to Louellen.''

Harry kicked back in his chair and, pouring himself another cup of coffee, settled in for a long talk with her. ''I haven't always been the housekeeper here, you know. I used to be a ranch hand. Did Jake ever tell you that?''

''No.'' Maggie wiped her eyes, feeling honored to be taken into Harry's confidence. She swallowed hard around the knot of emotion in her throat. ''What happened to make you change?''

Harry frowned unhappily, recounting, ''Jake fell apart when Louellen and the baby died. His sister Kelsey didn't know it, 'cause Jake managed to put on a good act whenever she was around. But the reality was he didn't eat, didn't sleep, didn't do anything but work himself into the ground. The ranch house went to ruin. Someone had to step in and make sure he had something to eat now and then, and push him into bed when he needed sleep but was too proud and stubborn to admit it. So I did all that.'' Harry sighed heavily, his own lament evident. ''But the one thing I could never make him do was talk about his loss, cope with it and grieve.'' Harry pinned Maggie with a mutually concerned look. ''No one's been able to do that, Maggie. And it doesn't take a rocket scientist to know that Jake's not going to recover fully from his loss until he does deal with it.''

Maggie was silent, thinking. What Harry had told her squared with everything she had already intuited. And it squared with Sabrina's predictions, too. ''You expect me to get him to own up to all he's feeling deep inside?'' she asked. It was a powerful responsibility.

Harry looked at her hopefully. ''I have the feeling if anyone could do it, you could.''

Maggie shook her head. She only wished that was so. ''You're overestimating my impact on him,'' she replied sadly. ''Vastly overestimating it, Harry.''

''No, I don't believe I am.'' Harry paused, clearly not about to give up on either Maggie or his boss. ''Jake didn't tell me where he planned to ride this morning, but I know where he went anyway. And so, Maggie, should you.''

MAGGIE DIDN'T KNOW why she let Harry talk her into it, but she did. And half an hour later, she was cresting a hill on the deep interior of the ranch.

To her relief, Jake was exactly where Harry had predicted.

And the scene was right out of Sabrina's crystal ball. Hat in hand, Jake was lingering before the two graves. Maggie dismounted from Buttercup and tied her to a tree.

As she opened the white picket fence surrounding the graves, Jake turned. ''What are you doing here?'' he demanded, an expression of supreme unhappiness on his face.

Maggie swallowed. ''I came to talk to you.''

Jake's expression turned even grimmer. ''Why?''

Maggie strode closer, her footsteps disappearing in the soft manicured grass. She stopped just short of him. ''Because I think you owe me more than this, Jake.''

His jaw, already rigid, tautened even more. "I never made any promises to you—"

Maggie felt like a gambler with her entire life's earnings placed on one high-risk bet as she fastened her eyes on his and reminded him softly and implacably, "But you did convince me to stay here and you did make love to me. Granted, that doesn't come anywhere near to constituting a commitment, especially in this day and age, but I have a feeling it was a big step for you, making love to me here, in the house you once shared with Louellen."

Jake swallowed. The brooding look was back in his eyes, as well as the hurt. "What's your point?" he asked gruffly.

Maggie drew a deep breath and furthered her risk to an unsettling degree. No matter what it took, she had to make him face the fact that his life was not over, too. "If your feelings for Louellen are what's keeping us apart," she told him gently, "then you need to explain this to me. As a gentleman, Jake, it's the least you can do."

"First off, I never claimed to be a gentleman, Maggie—"

"But you are a gentleman, deep down," Maggie interjected complacently, choosing to ignore the fact he'd gone deeper into his Wounded Bear mode than ever.

"Second, I don't talk about Louellen to anyone," Jake emphasized bluntly.

"Well, maybe it's time you did," Maggie retorted angrily, slapping her hands on her hips.

"Fine. You want to talk about it, then we'll do so, but we'll do so somewhere else." Jake leapt onto his spotted Appaloosa and took off. Maggie had no choice but to climb on Buttercup and follow.

Jake rode hard. It was all she could do to keep up.

Some fifteen minutes later, they reached a stand of trees next to the meandering stream that cut across his ranch and fed the Guadalupe River. Jake dismounted wordlessly and led his horse to water. Still a little breathless, Maggie followed suit. Damn it all, if he had meant to show her exactly how difficult he could be, he was succeeding.

"You've got five minutes to ask anything you want." Jake guided his horse away from the stream, and tethered him to a tree.

Again, Maggie followed suit. Determined to get through to Jake one way or another, she made sure Buttercup was well-situated before she turned to him again. "I want the whole story, Jake."

He regarded her impatiently. "What do you mean, the whole story?"

"I want to know about your life with Louellen, where and when you met, *everything* up until the point she died." Her voice dropped a compelling notch. "I want to know how and why you became so hurt and disillusioned that six long years later, you have yet to recover."

Again, he turned away from her, a haunted look in his eyes.

"I mean it, Jake." Maggie threw down the gauntlet at long last, knowing that Harry was right—Jake had to talk about this, if he was to recover and move on with his life. And to that end she was willing to pull out all the stops to accomplish her goal. She stepped closer, her glance determined. "So either you tell me," she vowed, very low, "or I'll find someone else who will."

JAKE SWORE vehemently beneath his breath. He didn't know whether he was mad as hell at Maggie for following him here, or glad she had followed him; he had only known that she would find a way to be with him as soon as she had found out from Harry where he'd gone. He whirled on her, half wishing his anger at the world would do them both a favor and chase her away.

"You're determined not to make this easy on me, aren't you?" he demanded.

"And with good reason," Maggie replied, looking more tranquil than ever. "Everyone else has made it easy on you, Jake, and it's clear it hasn't helped. Instead, it may have exacerbated the situation to an unhealthy degree."

As much as Jake wanted to, he couldn't disagree with that.

Maggie leaned against a tree, and swept off her flat-brimmed hat. Her voice as gentle and soothing as a silk ribbon against his skin, she asked, "How long were the two of you together?"

Considering the depth of Maggie's determination, Jake figured they might as well get this over with. Once she heard the entire story and realized, as he did, that he was not likely to ever get over what had happened, he figured she would probably want to leave anyway.

With a beleaguered sigh, Jake began his recitation in a low, listless voice. "Louellen and I met in high school and married about a year after my dad died, when I graduated from college. It was rough at first. The ranch was on the verge of bankruptcy, but Louellen never complained. For the first five years, she held down two jobs—one on the ranch and one in town—and so did I. It was rough but we finally paid off all the debts and most of the mortgage on the ranch. With the cattle operation in the black again, I knew it was finally time for us to start a family of our own.

"Louellen wanted that, too, but she had some reservations about the timing. She wanted to wait until we had more of a nest egg in the bank, but I was young and idealistic, and I didn't want to put it off any longer. So I kept pitching the idea until she gave in."

He swallowed and had to force himself to go on guiltily. "As luck would have it, she got pregnant right away. She was so happy then—we both were." His voice trailed off sadly. Remembering was almost more than he could bear.

Still listening intently, Maggie searched his face. "And then what happened?" she asked softly.

Jake ran a hand over his face, as if that would take away some of the sorrow in his heart. "She was about two months along when the doctors discovered she had cancer. She learned it was invasive, there was little hope of her surviving, the most they could do was prolong her life a year or two, but she couldn't take the chemo or radiation without harming the baby. And she wanted the baby. God, how she wanted the baby." Jake's eyes grew moist. His voice grew hoarse. "She knew how much I wanted the baby. She didn't know how little time we had and she didn't want anything to spoil our joy. So she made her doctors keep her illness a secret from me until she could no longer hide it.'' He shook his head in an agony of regret. ''Once I found out, I pleaded with her to take whatever treatment was offered, anything to prolong her life, but Louellen was adamant. She was five months along by then and she was determined to give me our child as a token of our love. She was determined to leave something of the two of us behind and she told me, come hell or high water, our baby was going to be born alive.''

Jake swallowed again, and forced himself to continue. ''Meanwhile, she got weaker and sicker with every day that passed. When she was in her sixth month, the doctors knew they had to go ahead and deliver the baby by C-section if the baby was to have any real hope of surviving.''

Jake leaned against the tree, recalling the utter lack of joy surrounding what should have been one of the happiest moments of his life with his wife. ''Louellen agreed to the C-section,'' he reported numbly. ''And she was so happy afterward, even though she knew she was dying, because she knew she was leaving me with our child and that I wouldn't have to go through her death alone.'' Jake blinked rapidly as the tears rose in his eyes and his chest tightened to the point he could barely breathe. Turning his glance toward the sun-swept horizon, Jake said, ''She died several days after our daughter was born.''

''Oh, Jake,'' Maggie said, the heartache he felt mirrored in her voice.

Jake knew if he let himself fall apart now, he might never put the pieces of his life together again, so instead he began to pace as he recounted as impassively as he could, "Our daughter lived on for three more months. And during that time she suffered just about every problem premature babies can suffer." Jake drew a deep breath and clenched his teeth. "She had innumerable operations and procedures. Every day, I went to the hospital and I sat there with her and I hoped and I prayed for a miracle." Again, he had to pause. Had to avoid Maggie's eyes and force himself to go on. "Only no miracle ever came, and when I had to bury our baby girl right alongside Louellen I wanted to die right along with them." Because he had known somehow he had failed them both. Louellen, in pushing her to get pregnant, and perhaps exacerbating her illness in the process. And their daughter, in not saving her mother.

"Oh, Jake," Maggie whispered, stricken.

But Jake didn't want her pity.

"I didn't die, of course, but I did make myself a promise," he said stonily, balling his hands into fists. "I promised myself that I would never let myself be hurt that way again, because I knew I just wouldn't survive it. So I became a Good Time Gus with women. And that was it. Since then," he said simply, "I have spent all my time and energy building up my businesses and taking care of the ranch." And it had helped. It had kept him sane.

Maggie was quiet. He could tell by the look on her face she didn't know what to say. But then he hadn't imagined she would. What did you tell someone who had failed his entire family? First, Louellen and the baby. And now even Kelsey and Clint, and in a round-about way, because he couldn't seem to handle them on his own, the twins. Like it or not, he had to face it, as much as he had once wanted it all, he was not cut out to be a family man. And Maggie, curse her stubborn heart, deserved the best.

Jake knew Maggie was thinking she could fix this for him, much the same way she had taken the situation with the twins in hand. Once again, he knew it wasn't so. Jake shook his head at her. "I know it hurts you, Maggie," he said gently, determined to present her with the truth, "and I'm sorry, but I've just got no place in my heart, no strength, to go through anything like that again." Or put anyone else through it, either.

Maggie closed the distance between them and touched his arm lightly. "You have to know the odds are against anything like that happening to you or your family again. It was just fate doing a number on you."

Jake drew a ragged breath and moved away from her. "The odds were against it the first time," he reminded her brusquely. "It happened anyway—and when it did, I let everyone down. My wife, because she felt she had to shield me, and our baby, because I didn't know what to do or say."

Maggie sighed. Her lips parted.

He held up a silencing hand before she could interrupt. "And don't hand me that line about us not getting more burdens than we can handle in this life, 'cause I've heard it all," he told her, the grief and guilt welling up inside him to a disabling degree. "And I don't believe it, not any of it, not anymore. 'Cause I sure had more than I can tolerate."

To his regret, Maggie looked more hurt and at a loss than he had ever seen her. It took her a moment to pull herself together. "So, what are you saying, Jake? Do you want me to leave the ranch?" she asked quietly at last.

Jake didn't know how to answer that, though he had a very good idea what she wanted him to say. That he had changed his mind and would marry again and have a family after all. "I don't know," he said curtly, figuring he owed it to her to be brutally honest about this, too. He let his gaze rove the loveliness of her upturned face and the shimmering compassion in her deep blue eyes, and knew even if he was all wrong for her, that he would never forget the way they'd made love and the unselfish way she had given herself to him, even when he hadn't deserved her.

"There's a part of me that wants to rip the face off any man who gets near you, and there's another part of me, an even stronger part, the noble part," he admitted, "that just wants to walk away from you before we get any more involved than we already are."

He shook his head at the shaken expression on her face. Finally, it seemed she was beginning to get the idea she couldn't help him. And that was the hell of it. No one could.

"I don't want to hurt you, Maggie," he confessed gently, "I never did." Even though he could see he already had wounded her—badly. He sighed, took off his hat, and shoved a hand through his hair. "That's why I kept trying to warn you away from me, by whatever means might work." Once again he forced himself to be brutally honest. He knew that was the only way to protect her from even more pain. "But I can't pretend that I can give you something that just isn't in me anymore." Ignoring the hurt in her eyes, he pushed on resolutely, "I know I shouldn't have made love to you—I've known it all along—and I'm sorry about that, because I know it gave you hope that things might work out otherwise." He paused regretfully. "But now you know the truth."

The question was, he wondered, his heart twisting in pain, what was she going to do with it?

MAGGIE KNEW Jake wanted her to turn tail and run, after all he had told her. Knowing she needed a man she could depend on to be there through thick and thin, if she was going to have the fulfilling marriage and loving family of her own she so badly wanted, she knew that would be the wise way to proceed.

But that did not take into consideration the fact she was deeply, irrevocably in love with Jake, or the fact that she sensed more than anything right now, that he just needed a little space, a little time to think about what he was giving up by continually pushing her—and indeed everyone else—away.

Given what Harry had told her, the mere fact he'd talked to her about his loss had been a giant step. She just had to give him time, and follow that first step with others. But not too fast. Because, she was sure, to push him too hard right now, would be to lose him.

And that she didn't want.

Aware that a weight had been lifted off her heart as well, by his halting confession, his trust in her, Maggie followed Jake's lead and remounted. Together this time, she and Jake rode back to the ranch house at a sedate, leisurely pace. And though Jake was still thoughtful, almost excessively quiet at times, Maggie noted with relief that the tension lines around his mouth and eyes seemed a little less prominent.

As they drew up to the barns, a long stretch limo pulled up to the ranch house. Maggie gaped in astonishment as a uniformed chauffeur got out to open the doors.

Still sitting astride Buttercup, she looked over at Jake. "Tell me, please, you haven't arranged yet another date for me."

To her relief, Jake looked equally surprised by their monied visitor. "Not this time," he affirmed.

"Not ever again," Maggie murmured.

Jake's brows rose in silent inquiry.

"I've decided I want to find my own beaus from now on," Maggie said. Whether she and Jake ended up together or not—and she still hoped mightily they would overcome all the odds and end up together—she was not going to allow him to play matchmaker for her any longer, even if it did have the short-term advantage of making him jealous as all get-out.

Jake tried but failed to retain his impassive expression. "Fine with me," he said, shrugging, then narrowed his gaze at their unexpected guests. "Who the heck is that?" Jake asked, blinking at the sight of a dazzling woman and a little boy.

Maggie might have been upset had she not known—the woman was so incredibly lovely—but she did know her. "Oh my gosh, it's my friend Clarissa and her son Tommy!" Maggie said, amazed.

"Did you know they were coming?" Jake dismounted then gallantly offered Maggie a hand down from the saddle.

Maggie shook her head no as she placed both her

hands on his shoulders, for balance, and swung herself around. "But something must be up," she told Jake seriously as her booted feet touched the ground, and she held on to him a moment longer, regaining her equilibrium. "Because Clarissa doesn't do anything like this on a whim."

## Chapter Twelve

"That's some ring you've got there, Clarissa," Maggie remarked as she finished applying sunblock to all three boys and then gave them permission to get in the boot-shaped swimming pool.

"I know. Isn't it gorgeous?" Smiling happily, Clarissa held it out to catch the light. The huge, exquisite diamond sparkled. "I told Fred he didn't have to be quite so extravagant, but he insisted."

Maggie could imagine how exciting this was for her friend, who'd had to pinch pennies all her life. To be suddenly living the jet-set life thanks to her new fiancé, must be like a dream come true. "Fred's given you and Tommy a lot, hasn't he?" Maggie observed as seven-year-old Tommy, Rusty and Wyatt bobbed around happily in the shallow end of the pool.

Clarissa kept a careful eye on the boys as she stretched out on the chaise and sipped her iced tea. "Even this whirlwind trip to see you was Fred's idea," she confessed, smiling. "I talked about the fact Tommy hadn't seen you in so long and how I longed just to be able to spend the day with you from time to time, and the next thing I know he's flying me to

Houston. Your brother told me where to find you. Oh, Maggie, Fred tries so hard to make my every wish come true!''

"Fred's a great guy. So's Conor!'' Clarissa's son Tommy stated emphatically as he dashed out of the pool long enough to collect an inner tube.

Maggie lifted a curious brow. "Conor James is the baby-sitter I told you about,'' Clarissa explained as Tommy hopped back in the pool.

"Tommy certainly seems attached to him.''

"He is. Unfortunately,'' Clarissa sighed with heart-felt regret as she confided, woman to woman, "He's also the sexiest man I've ever met.''

"And that's a problem?'' Maggie teased, picking up on the undeniably excited glint in Clarissa's eyes.

"Yes,'' Clarissa replied emphatically, "since Conor is most definitely *not* what I am looking for.''

Nevertheless, Conor James did elicit quite a reaction from Clarissa, Maggie noted.

Looking reluctant to interrupt, Harry stepped outside, smiled at both women, and handed Maggie a message. "Jake said this call came for you.''

Maggie glanced at it, folded it and tucked it into the front of her swimsuit. "Thanks, Harry.''

"If you like, I can bring a phone out,'' Harry offered.

"No. That's okay.'' Maggie waved the offer aside. "I'll talk to Peter whenever.''

"Peter Lassiter?'' Clarissa asked, after Harry had gone inside the house.

Maggie nodded.

"I thought you quit modeling.''

"I did.'' Maggie sighed, her frustration with that

situation growing. "But you know Peter." Clarissa had met Maggie's lady-killer agent several times when visiting her in New York. "He keeps calling me, trying to entice me to come back to work, at least for another year or two."

Clarissa shrugged. "Would that be so bad? You could make several million more dollars in that time."

Maggie held up a hand. "I have enough money, Clarissa. More than enough to last me a lifetime. What I *need* is a good man in my life."

"And you think you've found him here in Texas," Clarissa ascertained casually.

As Maggie thought about Jake, and all they could mean to each other, her heart filled with warmth and love. "I know I have," she said softly. "I just have to convince him of that."

And, as Sabrina had said, Maggie reminded herself firmly, she had to mend Jake's broken heart first. If she could do that…if the future Sabrina had seen in the crystal ball was true…then Maggie's reward would be half a dozen children with the man she loved with all her heart and soul.

Clarissa shook her head at Maggie. When it came to matters of the heart, her old friend Clarissa and her cousin Hallie both read Maggie like a book. "I suspect we're now talking about Jake MacIntyre," Clarissa teased.

"You guessed right. But enough about me," Maggie said. "Let's talk about you. Are you sure this marriage to Fred is the right thing for you and Tommy?" As far as Maggie could tell, it had happened awfully fast. And not necessarily for all the right reasons.

"Why would you ask that?" Clarissa queried, a little defensively, able to see as clearly as Maggie where this was going.

"I don't know." Maggie shrugged. "I just...I have this feeling that if you took away the perks, your romance with Fred is not all you had hoped it would be." And that worried Maggie. A lot!

"I'm not a child anymore, Maggie," Clarissa insisted.

"I know."

"I have to do what is right for Tommy and me," Clarissa insisted.

"By that you mean be practical?" Maggie clarified.

"Of course."

Still keeping an eye on the three boys playing merrily but safely in the pool, Maggie took a long sip of her cool iced tea. "And your new baby-sitter, what does he think about this?"

Clarissa slanted Maggie an exasperated look. "I don't want to talk about Conor James."

Maggie studied her.

Clarissa folded her arms in front of her. "He thinks he knows what is best for me and Tommy. He doesn't. What Tommy needs is the same thing I needed when I was growing up. A secure home. No worries about where his next meal is coming from. When I marry Fred Tannenbaum and Fred becomes Tommy's father, he'll give Tommy so much. Things that I could never give Tommy in a million years."

And Clarissa would be sacrificing her own happiness to do so, Maggie thought. She frowned at her dear friend and warned, "Don't put too much store in money, Clarissa. It really isn't the key to happiness.

It's family that counts. Friends. Being with someone you love with all your heart and soul."

Because the rest, as Maggie well knew, didn't matter a gosh dang.

"CLARISSA AND TOMMY get off okay?" Jake asked several hours later, when he'd returned to the ranch house after an afternoon spent running errands and tending to ranch business.

Maggie nodded. "Their limo arrived to take them back to the airport about half an hour ago."

Jake frowned. "They could have spent the night here, you know," he pointed out.

Harry had suggested as much earlier, too. "I know," Maggie said with a sigh, "but Clarissa promised her fiancé she would be back in time to have dinner with him later this evening."

Jake studied her bluntly. "You're worried about her, aren't you?"

Maggie tried not to notice how handsome Jake looked in the white Western shirt and jeans. "That's nothing new, Jake. Clarissa, Hallie and I are as close as sisters and we've taken care of each other since we were kids."

"Speaking of Hallie," Harry said as he came into the kitchen to join them, "she called again, while you were out."

"Oh, no." Maggie threw up her hands in frustration. "I can't believe we keep missing each other." Maggie went to the phone, picked it up and quickly dialed Hallie's number. To her frustration, there was no answer on the other end.

"No answer?" Jake said, when she'd hung up. Maggie noted Harry was watching her, too.

"No." Maggie shook her head. And Maggie wanted to tell her about seeing Sabrina, to find out if Hallie had per chance seen the fortune-teller, too. "I'll have to try again later."

Jake nodded.

Their eyes met, held. Something was different about Jake, Maggie noted happily. It was clear he wasn't embracing the idea of marriage and children yet, but neither was he determinedly pushing her away as he had been earlier in the day.

That had to be a good sign. Didn't it?

"Unka Jake, Unka Jake, Mommy and Daddy are home!" Rusty and Wyatt came running in, waving their arms wildly. "They're here, they're here!" they yelled excitedly and promptly ran back outside.

JAKE STRODE to the car, flanked by Harry and Maggie. He had only to look at the happiness reflected on Clint and Kelsey's faces as they reunited with their twin sons to know everything had been patched up. He smiled his relief as Kelsey gave her sons a big hug and kiss and then engulfed Jake in a big hug, too. "Hi, big brother."

"Hey, Kelse. Clint." Still holding Kelsey in a one-armed hug, Jake reached over and shook his brother-in-law's hand. To his surprise, the gesture was returned warmly.

"We have some great news," Clint said with a smile, happily announcing to one and all, "I found a job as a ranch manager at a small but promising outfit in Colorado."

"The only thing is they need Clint up there right away," Kelsey interjected, looking as if this were a problem she was very happy to tackle, "so we've got to get moved, pronto."

Which meant—damn it all—Maggie no longer had a reason to stay. "You can stay for dinner, can't you?" Jake asked, a little desperately, and not just because, he realized reluctantly, he wanted to do a little family bonding.

Despite what he had said to Maggie this morning, he was not ready to let her go. Not anywhere near it.

"Afraid not." Oblivious to Jake's totally selfish motives, Kelsey turned down Jake's invitation with obvious regret. "We're going to pack up the boys and head back to Colorado with Clint."

"We're staying together from now on," Clint said firmly, as he encompassed Kelsey and the twins in a warm group hug.

"And there's something else," Kelsey said, a little less eagerly.

Clint looked at Jake, man to man. "I was wrong to be angry with you for getting me that job. I realize in retrospect you were only trying to help."

"Even so, I should have leveled with you," Jake said, accepting the apology in the spirit it was given, "instead of going behind your back. I promise I'll never do anything like that again."

"And I promise I'll never walk out on Kelsey and the boys again," Clint said.

Looking glad that was settled, Kelsey walked with Jake toward the ranch house. "So, how were the boys in our absence?" Kelsey asked.

"A handful," Jake said, as he laced an arm around

Maggie's shoulder, too. "But thanks to Maggie, Kelse," he reported happily, "we managed just fine."

"THEY SURE LEFT in a hurry," Maggie observed, half an hour later, as Jake's sister and her family waved and drove away.

"They had a lot to do," Jake murmured, aware he had a lot to do, too, if he did not want Maggie to leave, as well.

"I don't know about you two," Harry Wholesome said to Jake and Maggie, looking as if he knew Maggie and Jake had a lot to discuss—alone. "But I'm taking a well-deserved night off and going out to play poker with the guys."

"Have a great time. You've earned the break," Jake said cheerfully.

"In fact, now that I think about it, I'll take the whole rest of the weekend off and not come back until Monday," Harry decided, already heading for his quarters.

Ten minutes later, Harry had packed a bag and had left, too.

And for Maggie, the conclusion to her whirlwind stay on the ranch had all happened too fast. "I guess it's my turn now," Maggie said, as her eyes misted and her heart turned over in her chest.

Taking a deep breath, she started to step past him.

Jake moved to block her way. "Don't."

Maggie lifted her chin, unable to bear the onslaught of emotions she was feeling. Inside her was a tangled web of hurt pride and regret for a love that might never be, intense desire, and the unquenchable hope that dared him to overcome the odds and the obstacles standing in their way and simply change.

"Don't what?" she asked huskily, aware once again she was wearing her heart on her sleeve, and that it was his for the taking. And that she didn't care how long it took or what she had to give up, if only he would love her back with even one tenth of the intensity of feeling she felt for him.

"Don't leave," he said quietly.

Maggie's pulse throbbed in her neck. "I thought that was what you wanted," she replied quietly.

Regret sharpened the handsome features of his face. "I thought so, too, until it started to happen," Jake said, stepping forward and taking her in his arms. He ran his fingers lovingly through her hair. Tilted her face up to his, and rubbed his thumb across her cheek. He looked deep into her eyes, and in that instant, was more vulnerable than Maggie had ever seen him. "I don't want you to go," he whispered at last, as if he, too, were wearing his heart on his sleeve. "Not yet."

And maybe, Maggie thought, the eternal optimist, not ever? "Then I won't," she whispered back, lacing her arms about his neck. Not wanting him to feel pressured, she amended, "Not yet."

They studied each other in silence, aware they were on the brink. Happiness flooded through Maggie, and was mirrored in his dark eyes.

They hadn't solved anything yet, but they had taken that important first step. Jake was reaching out to her, not in frustration or anger, or overwhelming desire, but in tenderness and love. And that, Maggie thought, had to count for something.

AFTER THEY'D FINISHED a dinner of salad and grilled chicken, they took their wine into the living room and sank, side by side, on the sofa. "I can't believe the quiet," Jake said, marveling at the peace.

"I know." Maggie smiled and cuddled into the warm curve of his arm. "Remarkable, isn't it?" she said, as she rested her head on his shoulder. "It was one of the things I loved most after my brothers had left my care and all gone off to college." She sipped her wine slowly, loving the mellow feeling of just hanging out with him, because they wanted to be together. Loving the feel of him next to her, so warm and solid and strong. "Of course, holidays were different," Maggie continued, as Jake absently stroked the curve of her shoulder. "Then, things were as noisy and clamorous as ever. Noisier, actually," Maggie amended with a smile. "Everyone was so glad to be home."

Jake gently stroked her hair. "You love your brothers, don't you?"

Maggie nodded, as contentment seeped through her. "Very much."

Jake laid his free left hand over hers and twined his fingers with hers. "I meant what I said before. I'd like to meet them."

Maggie smiled, imagining that very well. "Perhaps one day you will."

"In the meantime…" Jake grinned. He took the wine out of her hand, put it aside. Standing, he helped her to her feet, murmuring, "Alone at last."

The low satisfaction in his voice…the promise of what was to come…had Maggie tingling from head to toe.

She liked that he had taken his time, spending the evening with her, instead of rushing her right to bed. Though now, it seemed, his patience in that area was exhausted. Which in turn, prompted Maggie to tease impishly, in her thick Southern drawl, "Why, Jake MacIntyre, you act as if you wanted this to happen." Admitting to herself all the while that she had been desperately wanting and waiting for this time together, too.

"You don't know how much," Jake murmured, bending his head to hers. He took her in his arms and kissed her, gently at first, then with sizzling intensity. The tenderness in his touch, coupled with his desire for her, kindled the hope that they would have a future together one day, if only she gave him time.

Wordlessly, Jake swept her up into his arms and carried her up the stairs, to his bed. In a move that was every bit as masterful as it was unnecessary, since they were quite alone in the ranch house for the entire weekend, he kicked the bedroom door shut with his foot, and carried her over to the bed and laid her down. Parting her knees with his, he braced a hand on either side of her and situated himself between her thighs. "Oh my," Maggie breathed. He had never behaved quite this way before.

"You're not supposed to say that yet," he teased, taking a wrist in each hand and slowly anchoring them above her head. "But you will," he promised, kissing her slowly, sensually and with breathtaking intensity. "When the time is right."

His promise made, he kissed her until their bodies melded in boneless pleasure. Dizzily, they stopped long enough to undress and come together once again.

She wanted to touch and caress him. To make this a mutual giving of pleasure, but he was insistent that he be the one in control, that he be the one whose hands and lips stroked down her body, again and again and again, until she twisted against him, no longer able to bear it. Until she shook with her need for him and made a low, whimpering protest. "Jake...Jake..."

"Now?"

"Yes. Yes." She was desperate to have him inside her, desperate for the intimacy to come.

Driven by the same frantic need as she, he paused only long enough to sheath himself in a condom and slide a pillow beneath her hips. They locked eyes and she opened herself to him, offering herself to him, heart, body and soul. Hoping that he did want a wife. Want her.

Taking everything she offered, giving her physically what he could not yet promise her emotionally, he lowered his mouth to hers once again and surged into her slowly, deliberately. Still kissing her passionately, he lifted her against him. She followed the pressure of his hands and arched against him as he entered and withdrew in repeated shallow strokes that soon had her breathing erratically and reaching for some distant, lofty point. Until he too lost the control he had imposed upon himself. And suddenly she was there. Shuddering in overwhelming release. And so was he.

After the lovemaking, he held her close, as unable and unwilling to untangle their bodies as she. And it was then that Maggie thought again about their future and recalled his earlier words. And she knew she had a promise to make to him, too. "One day, Jake, the time is going to be right for so many things," Maggie whispered lovingly, clasping him to her, as the after-shocks continued to tremble through her body and his.

Ignoring the doubts and fears that immediately surfaced in his sable eyes at any mention of the future, she wreathed her arms about his neck and pulled his head down to hers as she kissed him even more thoroughly. Feeling his immediate, powerful response, she promised with a confidence she could only hope was catching, "We're going to have everything, you and me. You'll see." Before they knew it, they'd be announcing their engagement in the Houston paper for all the world to see. And Maggie would at last have the life she had always dreamed.

# Chapter Thirteen

It had been years since Jake had taken off work for more than a few hours at a time. Spending all of Saturday evening, and all day Sunday talking, laughing and making love with Maggie was a revelation. He hadn't imagined he could enjoy so much leisure time, but he had, to the point he was tempted not to answer the doorbell when it rang at 7:00 p.m. Sunday evening.

Maggie looked at him and shrugged. "Ten to one, it's not for me," she drawled.

Jake hoped not.

Maybe it was selfish of him, but he did not want anyone intruding on the intimate paradise they had fashioned for themselves. The reality of their lives and disparate dreams would intrude soon enough. Right now, all he wanted to do was make love to Maggie again, and then hold her in his arms all night long.

The only thing was, the doorbell was for her.

"PETER!" Maggie threw her arms around the sandy-haired man's neck. In a white mesh and opaque maillot swimsuit that rivaled anything she had worn in her *Sports Illustrated* days, the hint of a day spent in the sun glowing in her skin and hair, Jake was reminded she'd had a fulfilling life before she met him, and would no doubt have one after she left. "For heaven's sake, what are you doing here!" Maggie exclaimed, as she enveloped their visitor in a warm Texas-style hug.

Ruining my evening, Jake thought jealously as he suffered through the quick cordial introductions Maggie made.

After shaking Jake's hand and, Jake thought, sizing him up, Peter let Maggie steer him into the living room. Peter sat on the sofa. Jake took an armchair. Maggie perched on the arm of Jake's chair and situated herself between the two.

Peter leaned forward earnestly. "I wanted to talk to you in person about that deal I made for you with Beautiful You Cosmetics."

Maggie put her hand on Jake's shoulder. "I quit modeling, Peter."

Peter smiled. "They don't believe you're serious and neither do I, which is why they are offering a cool three million for a two-year exclusive contract with you. You wouldn't have to do anything else, and they'd only require you to work three months a year."

"Right," Maggie replied with an ironic look at her former agent. "And those three months would actually be spaced out, maybe two days a week, for the entire two years. I'd have to go all over the country and Europe, too, wherever their cosmetics are sold, making personal appearances."

"So what?" Peter shrugged. "It's nothing you haven't done before and it would still give you five days a week free."

Maggie shifted her weight restlessly, the silky warmth of her thigh brushing Jake's arm in the process. "And if I happened to get married and pregnant in the meantime, what then?" she asked the New York deal maker.

Peter paused.

Maggie's hand tightened on Jake's shoulder and her blue eyes flashed. "There's a clause in the contract that makes it null and void if I do get pregnant, isn't there?"

"So what?" Peter replied. Unlike Jake, he had no problem with the idea of Maggie starting a family right away. "If you get pregnant, you can stop modeling for Beautiful You Cosmetics and start modeling maternity clothes."

Maggie rolled her eyes and regarded Peter with exasperation. "You don't give up, do you?"

Peter smiled persuasively. "Not on you, no, I don't."

"SO WHAT ARE YOU going to do?" Jake asked, the moment Peter Lassiter had left. The depth of his jealousy and possessiveness he felt for Maggie disturbed him. Technically, he knew this was none of his business, as he had no real claim on her. He also knew his feelings were not likely to change. So maybe he should get a claim. But what kind? She had already said she wanted everything he knew he would never be able to give to her...and he knew she would never be satisfied with less. Whatever happened, he did not want Maggie to be unhappy, and certainly not because of him.

"What do you think I should do?" Maggie asked.

Jake shrugged. As much as he wanted to influence her decision, he knew he had no right to do so, not with what little he was offering her. "It really isn't up to me, Maggie."

Briefly, disappointment glimmered in her eyes. He knew what she'd been hoping he would say—that he didn't want her to go. But he couldn't, not given the way things were. "I've got no right to stand in the way of what you want," he told her quietly.

Maggie knew she loved Jake in a way she had never loved anyone else, or ever would. There was a part of her that wanted to stay with him, on any terms. And another part of her that knew she deserved more than what he had offered her thus far, which was simply a very passionate and exciting love affair.

"So what are you going to do?" he repeated, coming closer.

Maggie knew Jake needed a wake-up call; maybe this was it.

"You heard me tell Peter I wasn't interested in the deal," she told him. And hoped—wished—he would show some relief. Instead, his expression remained remarkably impassive, under the circumstances.

"I also heard him say he'd call you in a few days," Jake remarked casually.

"That's just the way Peter operates," Maggie announced carelessly as she sashayed barefoot into the kitchen to start dinner.

Though Jake had changed into jeans and a shirt after their swim, Maggie seemed content to lounge around in a swimsuit. She continued, "He doesn't give up, on anything or anyone."

What about you, Maggie? Jake wondered. Do you

give up? Somehow the thought that she might keep trying to wear his resistance down when it came to marriage and children wasn't as daunting as it should have been. Especially given the fact he knew he was not going to change his mind in the end. He'd already given all he had to give. And it hadn't been enough. Just like it wouldn't be enough for Maggie.

"If you want to take the job, it would be okay with me," Jake said finally, forcing himself to be a lot more generous and understanding than he wanted to be, wishing like hell he did not feel so damn vulnerable where she was concerned. And yet somehow he knew this was not something that was going to change, either. She wanted to think he was just being mule-headed about this and would eventually change his mind. But a part of him feared his recalcitrance went much deeper than that.

"I don't need your permission, Jake," Maggie reminded him wryly. Her pulse racing, she took the makings for a salad out of the refrigerator and slammed the door with a shove of her foot, then paused to give him a pointed look. "Nor do I recall asking for it."

"You're right." Jake regarded her stoically, aware a reckoning of sorts had come all too soon. "I just thought you might want my blessing."

"I see." The impact of his words hit her like a sucker punch to the gut. Hurt and disappointment flickered across Maggie's face. "And you're giving it?" she asked tersely, her blue eyes suddenly glistening.

Considering what he was offering her, a temporary place to stay and an open-ended, no-strings affair, what right did he have to comment on anything she did? "I'm just telling you I won't mind, that it won't make any difference to me," Jake said, as he put two potatoes into the microwave. Hell, he thought, maybe it wouldn't be so bad, losing her to modeling, instead of another man. He could handle the thought of her working. Maybe even returning to see him from time to time.

Maggie stopped in the act of washing the lettuce leaves. She had to stay calm. Try to reason with him. Make him see what they'd be giving up. Her hands dripping water onto the countertop and floor, she regarded him wordlessly. It didn't take an army spy to see the war going on inside her.

"And I guess the clause forbidding me from getting pregnant works for you, too."

They had skated around the subject of babies effectively thus far this weekend, there was no more doing so. His expression rueful, he replied as gently and firmly as possible, "I told you I wasn't interested in marrying or having any more children, Maggie." His eyes held hers, reminding her he had not misled her about this, not in the least. Nor would he in the future. "I meant it," he said quietly, and would have given anything not to have seen the flash of hurt and devastation in her blue eyes.

Maggie shoved a hand through her hair. "Right." How could she have forgotten? Struggling to keep hold of her emotions she went back to washing lettuce leaves with swift, jerking motions. "But you are interested in making love to me."

He stepped in to help her. "Yes, I want to make love to you," he said, as they stood shoulder to shoulder at the double sink. Nothing had meant as much to him as the time they had spent together. The only time he felt truly and completely alive was when he was with her—in bed and out. Surely, no matter what else was wrong between them, she had to know that.

Maggie stiffened as they washed the last of the greens and put them into the spinner to drain. "I see," she said with a weariness that seemed to come straight from her soul.

Did she? Jake wasn't sure.

Determined she not think his attitude a careless disregard of her feelings on the subject, Jake turned her to face him, took her damp hands in his and searched her eyes. In a voice much more emotional than he would have liked, he told her quietly, "I can't pretend my outlook is the same as yours, Maggie, because it just isn't." He paused, struggling to curtail the avalanche of emotion that welled up inside him whenever this subject came up. "As much as part of me would like to, I can't go back to being the idealistic, hopeful man I once was, because I no longer trust in the happily-ever-after." And that, he thought, was putting it lightly. Because of what had happened to Louellen and their child, he had become, at heart, a pessimist in the extreme.

Maggie looked at him through a film of tears. "You could trust in the future, if you'd just try," she said thickly.

"No, Maggie," Jake told her sadly, knowing as difficult as it was for her to hear, that he was speaking only the truth. A part of him had died with his wife and child, a part that would never be resurrected, no matter how much Maggie or anyone else tried.

"I don't have it in me to marry again or risk having another child. Ever." He paused. Seeing the pain he was causing her, he tightened his hold on her fingers and struggled—this once—to put her needs and wants ahead of his own. "Knowing how much you want a family of your own, seeing what a fine mother you would make...part of me can't even blame you if you were to walk out on me now," he said with as much equanimity as he could manage.

"Part of you might even want that?" Maggie guessed.

Much as he wanted to, Jake knew he coudn't deny that he wanted to see her happy in ways he'd never be able to manage. "Maybe," he admitted honestly. He shook his head in heartfelt regret. "God knows I don't want to have to feel guilty about ruining your life, too."

Maggie blinked. "What do you mean, ruining?" she demanded, untwining her fingers from his, and jerking away from him. She regarded him with exasperation. "Who else's life did you ruin?" she demanded, not bothering to hide her annoyance with his relentlessly pragmatic view. "Louellen's?"

Jake braced his hands on his waist. Why deny what he knew in his heart to be true? "If I hadn't pushed her to get pregnant—" he began raggedly.

Maggie cut him off with a scoff of contempt; it was a short brittle sound. "Louellen wanted to have a family," she reminded him. "You told me yourself—you both did."

"I'm not denying that." Jake shook his head, railing at the familiar helplessness that welled up inside him whenever this subject came up. More uncomfortable than ever, he looked away from Maggie. Deliberately, he hardened his stance and his voice. "But I also can't deny the fact that if Louellen hadn't been pregnant at the time her cancer was discovered that she would have been able to take chemotherapy and radiation without worrying about the baby. Damn it, Maggie, don't you undrstand? If Louellen hadn't been pregnant—at my insistence, mind you—she might have lived."

"Listen to me, Jake." Maggie grasped his biceps tightly and forced him to face her. In a low voice, quavering with emotion, she said, "You have to stop punishing yourself for the death of your wife and daughter. I know you like to think otherwise—most of the men I know do—but you're not all-knowing and all-powerful. No one is. There was nothing you could have done that would've made the outcome any different, nothing you could have done to change things."

Jake was silent, knowing on one level that was true, and knowing on another, more deeply emotional plane, that the role fate might have played in this didn't mitigate the deep, relentless guilt and sorrow he felt, and would always feel.

Maggie brought her hands to his face. "Let me ask you something, Jake." Her touch grew gentle, compelling. "Would Louellen have wanted you to be miserable and alone the rest of your life?"

"No."

"What are the options, then?" Maggie continued bravely, dropping her hands and stepping back. She searched his eyes, allowing him no quarter. "Would she have wanted you to have a series of meaningless affairs, no matter how passionate?''

Jake released a sigh before admitting with reluctant honesty, ''Probably not.''

Maggie spread her hands wide as she surveyed him and shook her head. ''And yet you still feel guilty as hell, don't you, for having the audacity to continue to enjoy life, even after Louellen is gone,'' she said, upset. ''For actually enjoying going to bed with another woman.''

''I've never thought of it in that way,'' Jake responded, turning away. Knowing even as he spoke that wasn't exactly true. Since Louellen had died and he—who had expected to spend the rest of his life with his wife—had found himself on his own again, he had felt guilty every time he as much as kissed another woman. And heaven help him, even guiltier when it came to Maggie, because she made him forget all about Louellen when he was with her, because she had enticed him into making love with her, heart and soul, and no one else had even come close to doing that. Since Louellen's death, it hadn't mattered whether he was kissing or dancing with someone else, it was Louellen he was thinking about, Louellen he still loved. When he was with Maggie, it was just Maggie on his mind; there was no one else in the room with him. No ghosts of the past. Nothing but the present and the passion he felt. And that scared the hell out of him. Because it meant he was forgetting Louellen, and he had promised her before she died that that was the one thing he would never do.

''I told you I was still married in my heart and always would be,'' Jake turned back to Maggie and reminded her gruffly. Yet even as he spoke the angry words, he wasn't sure it was quite true anymore. The past twenty-four hours had changed things. The whole week with Maggie had changed things, to the point he knew they would never return to the way they had been.

"And yet you made love to me anyway, repeatedly," Maggie reminded angrily, looking as if she felt even more betrayed. "Not just once, but again and again and again." Her hands were balled into fists at her sides. She looked as if she wanted to deck him.

"Yes," Jake said. Knowing he could hardly blame her if she did deck him.

"Why, Jake?" Maggie asked hoarsely, the emotion in her low voice making him feel all the guiltier. "Why did you make love to me as if we were the only two people left on earth, if you were just planning to push me away in the end?"

*Because I need you in a way I can't begin to explain. In a way I'm not sure that I'm ready to understand,* Jake thought, on a troubled sigh. Knowing Maggie expected—deserved—some explanation, he said finally, "Because, God help me, I wanted you. Because I don't want to lose you."

And he knew, even before he had finished, what a lame, untrue excuse that really was. The way he'd made love to her had been anything but a calculated ploy. But it was too late.

Maggie glared at him in a way that let him know it would be a cold day in hell before she ever forgave him for this.

"Too bad, Jake," she snapped. "You already have."

"ISN'T THERE ANYTHING I can say to you to get you to change your mind?" Jake asked in exasperation, knowing this weekend was not going to have the end he had hoped.

"Short of getting down on your knees and begging, you mean?" Maggie asked sarcastically as she carried her clothes from the bureau to her suitcase. Having decided that staying for dinner was as pointless as pretending she and Jake had any kind of future at all, she had decided to cut her losses, and curtail her heartache, and leave right away.

"I'll even do that," he said, following her around. After doing everything he could to push her out the door and out of his life, Jake was practically begging her to stay.

Maggie peeled off her swimsuit and stepped into a pair of matching peach silk panties and bra. "But what you won't do is stop wallowing in self-pity and fear."

Jake glared at her. "If you think I'm going to apologize for being so in love with my wife and child that their death damn near killed me, you're wrong."

"I've never once belittled your loss and you know it," Maggie snapped, her cheeks hot with anger. "It's your unwillingness to look to the future that is killing me—killing us!"

Having no argument for that, Jake watched as she tugged on a pair of shorts and a T-shirt.

Maggie sat on the edge of the bed to put on her socks and tennis shoes. "Look, if you enjoy being the broken-hearted martyr, then so be it. As for myself," Maggie told him with a tranquility that appeared even more disturbing to him than her anger, "the way I look at it, is either you want to love me or you don't, either you want to get married and have children or you don't.''

And he, she thought, hurt beyond measure, obviously didn't. Worse, was the galling sense of déjà vu the whole sordid episode had for her.

Maggie marched over to her suitcase and slammed it shut. While he watched, she struggled ineffectively with the clasps. ''I've already been with a man who felt he was being hog-tied and dragged to the altar,'' she said, ignoring his low exasperated curse, ''and I'm not doing it again.'' Furthermore, she didn't care what he thought; as far as she was concerned, this love affair was over. ''I'm tired of giving you the benefit of the doubt,'' she raged on in the stony silence of the room, fighting not to cry. ''I'm tired of hoping against reality that things will change,'' she said as the hurt inside her built and built. '''Cause there's just no point to that,'' she stormed, giving him no chance to get a word in edgewise as she picked up her suitcase and staggered under the weight of it. ''It's all or nothing for me. And you, cowboy, have made your choice.''

BUT HAD HE? Jake wondered, just as emotionally. Or was she backing him into a corner with her demands, her insistence he do things her way or watch her hit the highway? ''Why do you have to leave now, this instant?'' he demanded, taking the ridiculously heavy suitcase out of her hand and putting it back on the bed.

''Because now that the boys are gone I have no reason to stay.''

''Except one.'' Jake regarded her stormily. ''The

fact I want you to stay." Surely that had to count for something.

"As what, Jake?" Hands planted on her hips, Maggie stared up at him in exasperation. "Mistress? Girlfriend? Live-in? Certainly not bride-to-be?"

As always, the thought of marrying again, of opening himself up to that kind of hurt, had Jake's gut clenching. Though if he'd want to marry anyone, if he wanted to have another child with anyone, it would be Maggie. Knowing he wasn't ready for that...knowing he might never be...knowing he also did not want her to leave...not now...maybe not ever, when it came right down to it, and it had... Jake said quietly, "How about staying here as my friend? How about we start slowly?" *Very* slowly. Instead of trying to wrap things up in a week's time. Surely *now* he was meeting her halfway.

But Maggie only shook her head. One look at her face told him she was tired of being strung along. "Not good enough, Jake," she replied flatly. "We'd *still* be going nowhere."

Jake couldn't argue the future, so he concentrated on the present, a present he wasn't anywhere near ready to give up, and damn it, before Peter What's-His-Name had shown up, neither had she.

Sensing from her recalcitrant expression that she was about to run out on him, with or without her suitcase, he clasped her shoulders and held her in front of him. "Friendship...and the start of a damn fine love affair...was good enough to keep you here last night and this morning," he reminded her.

Maggie's slender shoulders stiffened beneath his staying grip. "That was different," she stated, stepping back and away. Arms folded in front of her, she paced back and forth. "I didn't realize then how irretrievably stubborn and foolish you are. I do now."

The thought of a life without her was more than Jake could bear. He knew, too, that unless he offered more there was no chance on this earth she would stay. "What if we lived together for a while then?" he asked, desperate to keep her with him. "You know, have a trial run, and then if it works out, we could get married, at some point down the road?" Continuing to have her on the ranch with him was an idea that pleased him.

Maggie looked at him as if she had an idea what the halfhearted proposal was costing Jake. But she also seemed to think it wasn't good enough, for either of them, and never would be.

"Thanks, but no thanks, Jake," she said wearily.

His frustration erupted. "Why not?" Jake demanded, wishing she would make some attempt to meet him halfway, too.

"Because there's just no point in it." Maggie sighed and ran her hands through her mane of silky golden blond hair, before she continued in a low voice that was bleak and utterly defeated, "Besides, we've already shared space and simultaneously assumed care of and responsibility for Rusty and Wyatt and we know we get on fine, in that sense. We'd make great housemates, great parents, great lovers, even great husband and wife, assuming you were ready to take the leap," she told him, *"and you're not."*

Jake regarded her in frustration. He had never wanted not to lose something more in his life. He had also never wanted more not to let someone down. And that put him in one hell of a quandary. "And that's it?" He swore heatedly, aware that what he and Maggie had was very special, even if it wasn't anywhere near as permanent as she wanted it to be. "I don't meet each and every one of your demands, so you're leaving?" He regarded her incredulously. What had ever happened to accepting love as it came? To finding pleasure in the moment? To enjoying the beauty of a season before it ended?

Maggie shrugged and regarded him with a sorrow every bit as deep and all-encompassing as his own. "Despite what you would like to think, Jake, this is not going to get any easier, no matter how long we put it off," she said in a low voice that let him know she couldn't tolerate being in his presence one second longer. "So I'm going to do us both a favor and go now. Before this hurts either of us any more."

# Chapter Fourteen

"This is one situation where numbers will definitely not win the game for you," Maggie warned her brother, Billy, several days later.

"I don't know what you're talking about," Billy vowed as he strolled into the breakfast nook, where Maggie sat poring over the latest pages from her portable fax machine. Her friend at the *Houston Chronicle* had taken pity on her and was pulling out all the stops to help Maggie find a suitable mate. It wasn't going to be easy, replacing Jake in Maggie's heart; but she was determined to succeed. And since sheer determination had paid off many, many times in her life in the past, she was sure it would eventually help her now. That was, if she could get her three protective brothers off her case. Which at the moment did not appear very likely.

"Come off it, Billy." Maggie regarded him with a frown. "I know why you called Deke and Frank to come and talk to me this morning."

"And what reason might that be?" Deke asked, ignoring the testy set of her shoulders, and pulling up a chair.

Maggie sighed her exasperation loudly and paraphrased his objections adroitly, "You do not think I should be devoting all my energies to a husband hunt." Maggie scanned the list of Texas millionaires in front of her and, ignoring the fact that she couldn't conjure the slightest enthusiasm for meeting him, marked one as possible.

"You always were able to read my mind," Frank said, strolling in and sitting down, too.

"Particularly when you are still so clearly on the rebound," Billy added, pulling up the last chair.

Aware they were about to head into very dangerous territory—territory that could easily make her cry—Maggie tensed. "What are you talking about?" she demanded cooly.

Her three brothers exchanged troubled glances. Finally, Deke spoke. "It's pretty clear you're carrying a torch for Jake MacIntyre."

"I was," Maggie corrected loftily, circling another possibility for a mate, even though she considered his statistics hopelessly flawed, too. "I'm not anymore. What Jake and I had is well over."

"Technically, maybe," Deke said.

"In every way," Maggie corrected firmly. One by one, she gave each of her brothers a quelling look.

In response, her three brothers all shook their heads at her disparagingly. "Maggie, you may be able to fool everyone else, but you can't fool us," Frank told her gently. He curved a compassionate hand over her forearm. "We know you. We know how hard you fell for that guy. And to tell you the truth, the three of us have half a mind to hunt that rapscallion down and break both his legs."

Maggie grinned. It was the first time she had smiled all day. "Guys, come on," she reasoned with them

bluntly, knowing—as hot as their feelings were toward
Jake for hurting her so—that they were talking meta-
phorically. At least she hoped they were talking meta-
phorically. "Just cool it, okay?"

Silence rebounded in the breakfast nook. "Only if
you tell us you're going to be okay," Frank countered
quietly.

Maggie took a deep breath and through sheer force
of will, pushed back the tears she could feel gathering
behind her eyes. Part of her knew she was never going
to be okay again, not after loving Jake and losing him.
Was this how Jake had felt after losing Louellen and
the baby? Dear heaven, no wonder he didn't want to
risk having his heart broken into a million pieces
again. She couldn't imagine trying to love again, either.

Aware her brothers were watching her cautiously,
Maggie put on a stiff upper lip. "I'm going to be fine,
guys, really," she said as she picked up her marker
pen again.

"You promise?" Billy asked.

Maggie nodded solemnly. "I promise," she said, as
Deke, Frank and Billy all put their hands on top of
hers in the family symbol of unity. "I'm going to have
that husband and family of my own that I want, one
day soon, no matter what."

As for Jake, Maggie sighed, if he chose to live the
rest of his life alone, that was just going to have to be
his problem.

"HOW LONG ARE YOU going to sit around not speaking
or shaving?" Harry demanded of Jake Thursday morning.

Jake glared at Harry over the top of his morning

newspaper. "You bring that up one more time and how long before you find yourself looking for a new employer?" he countered archly.

Harry only grinned. Happy, no doubt, that he had at last provoked a verbal response, albeit a somewhat testy one, out of Jake, who hadn't been speaking much at all to anyone since Maggie had left the Rollicking M. "You weren't this bad after Louellen died," Harry stated.

Jake hadn't felt this bad, either. Which was odd, 'cause he'd never imagined anything could feel anywhere close to the gut-wrenching pain he had felt at Louellen's death. Yet here he was, miserable all over again, in a very different way. Maybe because Louellen had been so very sick, especially there at the end, and he'd known he was going to lose her. Maggie he hadn't expected to lose.

"'Course you were younger then, and more naive," Harry continued, removing Jake's untouched plate.

"Naive?" Jake echoed incredulously. What the hell was Harry talking about now?

"Yeah." Harry nodded solemnly as he rewarmed Jake's untouched eggs and bacon in the microwave. "Back then, you didn't know how hard it was going to be to go on year after year, completely alone, without a wife or kids of your own."

That was true, Jake thought, grimacing as he took a sip of the coffee he'd let cool to lukewarm. He looked at Harry pointedly. "You're one to talk. You never married or had kids."

"Because I didn't want either," Harry reminded, as he went about rewarming Jake's toast. "You did, Jake. Very badly, as I recall."

Deciding this conversation had gone far enough,

Jake put his paper down and gave Harry a warning glance.

"'Course you had forgotten all about that, until Maggie Porter came along," Harry continued with smug satisfaction as he set Jake's breakfast in front of him again. "Having her here kind of reminded you of all you'd been missing, didn't it? And you liked it...liked the excitement of having a wife and kids, even if the kids were temporarily on loan from your sister, and the wife...well, that was just playacting, wasn't it, Jake?"

"I didn't pretend anything," Jake retorted gruffly, forking up a mouthful of eggs. That was the problem. He'd been too damn honest with Maggie. He'd known it was a mistake to tell Maggie—to tell any woman—anything. No one in their right mind would want to be a living, breathing replacement for his late wife. And Maggie Porter was a woman very much in her right mind. No wonder she had left him. Under the circumstances, he could hardly blame her.

"Then you did care about Maggie," Harry ascertained.

Jake released an exasperated breath. "Of course I cared!" That had never been in question!

"Just not enough." Harry poured Jake some more juice, and handed it over.

"Enough for what?" Beginning to feel a little claustrophobic in the spacious ranch house kitchen, Jake downed his juice in two long, thirsty gulps.

"Good question." Harry applauded Jake with an approving look. "Enough to make her want to stay?"

Jake swallowed, his heart aching as he admitted reluctantly, "She did—"

"Really?" Harry looked downright amazed.

"Yes," Jake affirmed, irritated beyond belief that Harry could think Maggie's love for Jake was so far out of the realm of possibility. "She did."

Harry narrowed his eyes at Jake contemplatively, his disapproval growing by leaps and bounds with every second that passed. "And yet you forced her out, the same way you've been forcing everyone out of your life, since you lost Louellen and the baby."

No one had to remind Jake what a jerk he had been, in ever allowing Maggie to get tangled up with him in the first place. Nor did anyone have to remind him how lonely he had been since she had left. "What do you want from me?" he asked Harry impatiently. He followed that with an irritated glare.

Harry flattened his palms on the kitchen table and leaned over Jake. "I want the same thing Maggie and everyone else who loves you wants," he told Jake gruffly. "I want you to wake up. I want you to grieve. Openly, this time. I want you to do whatever you have to do to get your life back on track."

Jake gave Harry a black look. "And then?"

"And then it's up to you," Harry said simply. He paused, making sure he had Jake's full attention. "You can go after Maggie, and prove to her that you love her, or you can spend the rest of your life wishing you had done the same. The choice, Jake, is up to you."

"YOU ABOUT READY?" Billy asked Maggie, early Saturday morning.

"Yeah." Maggie knelt to tie her running shoes. "How far are we going to run?"

"I'd like to get in at least six miles."

Maggie groaned. Her brother, the football player

turned coach, had always been able to run her into the ground. "Billy, I can't do six miles."

Billy, who planned to shower and shave after their early morning run, thoughtfully ran his hand along his bewhiskered jaw. "Well, what is comfortable for you?" he asked.

"Two, maybe." *Maybe.* She doubted even then she would be able to keep up with Billy.

Billy grinned and slipped his coach's whistle around his neck. Hands on his hips, he looked her up and down. "I can see I've got my work cut out, whipping you into shape, sis."

"Very funny. And don't you dare even think about blowing that whistle at me," Maggie warned as his doorbell rang.

They looked at each other. Maggie knew they felt exactly the same urge to slip out the back way and let whoever it was wait. But, since it was football season, and Billy'd had a slightly injured player in the game the evening before, a contest his team had won hands down, they couldn't do that. "I'll get it," Billy said. "And then we'll head out for the track."

Maggie nodded, and went to the sink to fill their water bottles. She heard the muted murmur of deep male voices; whatever was going on sounded very serious indeed. Then, Billy's voice, loud and distinct, summoning her. "Sis, can you come here a minute?"

Maggie set the water bottles down and strode out into the terra-cotta entry way. Catching sight of their unexpected guest, she stopped dead in her tracks. Her breath stalled in her lungs at the sight of him. "Jake—"

"I know. I should have called," he said.

"My inclination was simply to throw him out," Billy explained grimly.

"That would be mine, too," Deke and Frank said, joining them. Both were also in their jogging clothes. "Particularly if this is who we think it is, the guy who hurt you."

"It is," Maggie said quietly, her eyes still holding Jake's. So hungry for the sight of him was she, after only six days, that she could not take her eyes from him, nor he from her. It was clear he had showered and shaved with care that morning. He was wearing a dark blue Western shirt, black jeans and a black silk gambler's vest. He had a bouquet of yellow roses, what appeared to be Billy's morning paper and black Stetson in hand.

"I was hoping to get here after you'd already read the paper," Jake began, ignoring her brothers and concentrating completely on her. "I thought it might make getting started a little easier."

Considering the way their affair had ended, Maggie didn't for the life of her see how.

"But in any case, I want you to look at this, too." He handed her a manila envelope.

Maggie opened the clasp, withdrew the papers inside. "Engagement, wedding and anniversary announcements," she read out loud. "Policy and procedure." She looked at Jake, not sure what this meant. "Why are you giving these to me?" she asked thickly. She'd thought she was finished with him, and he her. She'd thought they'd never see each other again.

"Because you're going to need them, if you want all of these dreams of yours to come true," he said firmly.

She didn't know whether to be glad or sad. She only

knew everything that had ever mattered to her hinged on the next few moments of her life. She swallowed hard. "Is this a game, Jake?" she asked finally. If so, her brothers were going to be very mad. As was she, gosh darn it.

"No, Maggie. No more games. No more playing around, for either of us. I know what I want," he told her firmly, taking her by the shoulders.

The heat and gentleness of his touch sent tremors sizzling through her.

"The question is," he continued, "do you?"

Yes, Maggie thought, with all my heart and soul.

His eyes still holding hers, Jake dropped his hands and inclined his head toward the newspaper in her hand. "Open it up to the life-style section," he prodded.

Realizing Jake looked different somehow…better…in some mysterious way, Maggie swallowed around the sudden dryness of her throat and, against her better judgment—hadn't he hurt enough already?—wordlessly did as he asked.

"What's on there?" Deke asked, looking over her shoulder, along with Billy and Frank.

"It's a full-page ad," Maggie replied, shocked and struggling to take it all in. For in large block letters, the newspaper print said simply, "Maggie, I love you. Not just for today or tomorrow, but for the rest of my life. So there's only one thing to do. You've got to marry me. Jake."

JAKE WAITED, watching Maggie's face. It was impossible to tell what she was thinking. He could only pray it wasn't too late as she turned to her brothers and said quietly, "Why don't you-all go jogging without me this morning?"

Deke, Frank and Billy exchanged glances of mingled hope—that everything might work out for their sister after all, she guessed—and concern.

"I don't know about this," Deke said finally, still looking as if he wanted to deck Jake.

"Please," Maggie said, folding her arms in front of her and looking even cooler and more composed. "Jake and I have a lot to discuss," she continued crisply, "and these are the kinds of things that need to be said in private."

"All right," Deke finally consented reluctantly. "But we'll be at the high school track if you need us."

"Yeah," Billy said, scrawling a phone number on the notepad. "And don't hesitate to call my office—they'll find me." He turned to Jake and gave him a warning glare. His brothers followed suit. "You be good to her."

"Don't worry," Jake assured them, "I will be."

"Really, guys, I'll be fine," Maggie emphasized flatly.

Finally convinced of it, her brothers left.

Jake breathed a sigh of relief. Knowing she would tell him as soon as she'd decided, he lounged against the front hall bannister and waited for her decision.

She fingered the proposal in the newspaper. She gave no clue as to what she was feeling on her face. "This is a pretty flamboyant gesture." One that would, no doubt, cause them no end of infamy in this state.

Jake drew a breath and nodded agreeably.

Clad in a T-shirt and running shorts, her blond hair

drawn up in a high, bouncy ponytail, Maggie looked much as she had at the ranch. Recalling how he'd taken her presence for granted then, Jake felt a stab of pain. He promised himself if he ever got another chance with her, he would never take her for granted again.

His dark eyes lasered in on her upturned face as he replied laconically, "I figured it'd have to be a pretty flamboyant gesture to get your attention and persuade you to forgive me, after everything I put you through."

Maggie folded the paper and put it aside. Leaning against the opposite wall, she folded her arms in front of her, and continued to regard him warily. "Do you mean it, Jake?" she asked in the soft, serious voice he had come to love. "Do you really *want* to marry me?" she pressed emotionally, moisture glimmering in her wide blue eyes. "Or are you just going through the motions because you've been roped into it, because I wouldn't be with you again any other way?"

About this, Jake had absolutely no doubt. "I mean it," he said gruffly. "I want you to marry me."

To his dismay, she still remained unconvinced. "What happened to change your mind?" Maggie demanded, and he knew from the look on her face that his answer had better be good.

"I realized the moment you left the Rollicking M Ranch that without you, life on the ranch was just life on the ranch. I want you back, Maggie. I want you to be mine. I want to have babies with you and take all the risks I've been afraid to take."

The words Maggie had been longing to hear filled her heart with joy. Tears of happiness misting her eyes, she went toward him, arms outstretched. He wrapped her in his arms. She clung tightly.

"Oh, Jake," she whispered, relief and wonder flowing through her in waves. Her devastation at leaving him had been so great, she had almost given up hoping this would happen. To find it had, brought a bliss almost more than she could bear. Contented moments passed as they simply held each other.

Finally, Jake whispered in a rusty-sounding voice, "I'm sorry, Maggie. So sorry I hurt you. Sorry I was such a fool."

"I'm sorry, too." Aware she was as much at fault as he was, Maggie clung to him as he lovingly stroked her hair. "I shouldn't have pushed you so hard," she confessed softly.

Jake drew back to look into her face. "No, you were right to do that," he said seriously as he gently caressed her face. "If you hadn't...well, who knows how long it would have taken me to snap out of it?"

"But you have, haven't you?" This was what was different about him, she realized with a belated sense of relief. The edgy mantle of grief he'd worn was gone.

He nodded. "I realized, after a lot of thought, that maybe you and Harry were right. Maybe all this time I hadn't let myself grieve. Maybe my delayed grieving, more than fear, was the reason that I couldn't get involved with anyone else. I couldn't give my heart to you as completely as I wanted to because I hadn't really shut the door on my marriage to Louellen."

"But now you have?" Maggie asked.

"Yes." Jake looked at her with quiet confidence. "I finally feel that part of my life is over. Louellen would want me to go on, every bit as much as you do, Maggie." He paused to pull a small velvet box from his pocket. "So, if it isn't too late, if you'll still have me, I want you to stop looking for someone else to embody all the qualities on your wish list and marry me and have my—our—children."

Maggie grinned appreciatively at the diamond-and-sapphire engagement ring she found inside the box. She couldn't believe it, but all her dreams were coming true. "Not to worry, Jake. My days of husband hunting are over because I love you and only you." She removed the ring and slid it on the ring finger of her left hand. It was a perfect fit. Just as Jake was the perfect man for her. "And as for my list—"

"Yes?" Jake lifted her hand to his lips and kissed it tenderly.

Maggie ran her fingers through his dark windswept hair and looked deep into his eyes. "I won't be needing that anymore, 'cause I've found what I was looking for in you."

"Sure?" Jake teased.

Maggie nodded, confirming, "You're the quintessential cowboy."

"And even if I'm not," Jake drew her nearer and kissed her slowly, thoroughly. "It is definitely something to work on."

Knowing how insatiable he could be in that regard, Maggie grinned and teased, "In bed and out?"

"Maggie honey," Jake drawled, sweeping a hand down her spine, "you read my mind."

They kissed some more, until Jake finally drew back long enough to ask, "When can we tie the knot?"

Maggie's lips curved in sweet anticipation. For her, it literally could not be soon enough. "How about yesterday?" she said, laughing.

Jake cheerfully considered her suggestion. "Sounds good to me," he drawled, and they kissed again.

"I can't wait to tell my brothers," Maggie said a long contented time later, as he held her close and she drew lazy patterns on his chest. "Hallie and Clarissa, too."

Jake clasped her hand and held it over the strong, steady beat of his heart. "Hallie is still trying to reach you, by the way," he remarked amiably.

Maggie sighed, frustrated. "It's been one of those weeks where all we do is play telephone tag. I'll try her again in a little bit."

Jake paused. "Think she'll be surprised you're going to marry a cowboy?"

"She'll be ecstatic," Maggie confirmed. "So will Clarissa. They'll be even more amazed when I tell them Sabrina—that fortune-teller I told you about— saw you in her crystal ball."

Jake entwined their hands. "I've never been one to believe in anyone's ability to foresee the future—" he started to say skeptically.

"Me, either," Maggie agreed. "But if Sabrina is even half right, then my friend Clarissa and cousin Hallie are both really in for it, too." Maggie grinned as she stood on tiptoe, wreathed her arms about his shoulders, and gave Jake another long, lingering kiss. "I only hope they're as happy as we are, Jake," she murmured finally.

He hugged her close, letting her know with the tender protectiveness of his touch that they had their whole lives ahead of them, and this time, nothing would force them apart.

Smiling, Jake bent and kissed her again. "Me, too."

# THIRTY.
## SINGLE.
### ON A HUSBAND HUNT.

Clarissa, Maggie and Hallie have their practical reasons for attempting to override fate. And they're not leaving anything to chance!

- They selected eligible bachelors.
- Did their research.
- Consulted their lists and spreadsheets, their bar graphs and flow charts—even double-checked with a wizened soothsayer, just to be sure— before they narrowed it down to:

√ a <u>millionaire</u>   √ a <u>cowboy</u>   √ <u>the boy next door</u>

But will a roguish millionaire, a genuine Texas cowboy and the boy next door show these little ladies that you just can't forgo passion for tidy emotions?

## How To Marry...

**A MILLION-DOLLAR MAN**
Vivian Leiber
(March)

**ONE HOT COWBOY**
Cathy Gillen Thacker
(April)

**THE BAD BOY NEXT DOOR**
Mindy Neff
(May)

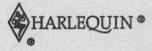

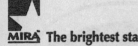

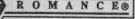